MW01241014

The Bl

Through the Eastern Door

The Black Robes

by Bishop Feeney
with Alley Rice

Saint Kateri Tekakwitha

Born 1656 and died 1680 at age 24

Dedication

Isaiah Makonnen,
always in our thoughts
and our hearts.

Contents

Prelude

In the beginning of time, the First Nation established itself as a force of power and defined the honor of family life. As the centuries began to roll by, life stayed the same amongst the native tribes. Then they began seeing new people coming to their shores in all manner of transportation, dressed in everything from rough skins to the lace and finery of the greatest European cities of Paris, London, Amsterdam, and of course Madrid. While these were just a few of the interlopers' ports of call, they became the most influential and powerful in the newly rediscovered lands. The Spanish came, with their divine horses running swiftly along the well-worn trails trampled by the natives. They swept across the southlands and pillaged much of what they discovered. Their mission was to establish a foothold in this exciting discovery of well-forested and incredibly well-stocked rivers and streams, with their bounties of fish and small game along their banks. It was all theirs for the taking, and everything they deemed worthy of the king and country was within their grasp.

Long before all others, the Vikings first landed where they met a force as great as theirs. The small band of voyagers probably never made it back to Iceland after finding a congregation of men in feathers and skins equal to their ferocity and ready, willing, and able to defend their homeland fires. Then, as in all eras of man's history, lingering sickness and the need to find faster, more profitable passages to the trade cities brought the expansionism and sheer disrespect for those they encountered. A flag appropriately placed here or there, a map drawn with the finest of detail, and strength of the quill claimed great holdings for those who first came as adventurers and explorers. They came but never conquered the peoples of the woodlands, and they began to eliminate them or traveled far from their villages to avoid the conflicts whenever possible.

They were greeted with friendship but ended up being rebuffed as they began to greedily strip this land of its greatness, seemingly as quickly as a wildfire claims a hillside. The natives who inhabited these lands were willing to trade with the men and sign agreements of peace and trade, yet they likely knew nothing of the documents' contents or consequences to their way of life. They were a trusting and pure people, almost childlike in their dealings of daily life. The search for the mineral riches turned quickly to the discovery of great herds of deer and elk, and then to the industrious beaver along with the pelts of all the furbearers. The easily netted cod abounded on the northern shores of the discovery, and the swift cold rivers produced the smelts, trout, and alewives.

As the years wore on, so did the conflicts between the discoverers. As the strife of unprotected borders spread, so did the need to bring their religions to the new worlds. The French brought the friars and monks to Canada, and they moved among the villages of first the Algonquin and then other eastern tribes. Eventually, they began to follow the trappers to the sparsely populated native villages to spread their god's word. One such village was Ossernenon, in what today is Fonda, New York. Here, the missionaries met with defiant natives who did not want their lives changed in any way, except for a few of the women who had been captured earlier in native conflicts. Many such missionaries were left without a flock and were generally ignored. Then, as time passed, the French established small chapels in the villages and came to live among them. Now, slowly, they began gaining their trust.

One young native girl, Kateri Tekakwitha, daughter of the chief, embraced this new way and began to seek out the answers the monks brought with their sermons. She became devout and lived the way of the Bible, constantly striving to learn more of its secrets, and came to embrace the concepts that unfolded. She lived a pure life without the benefit of a husband and bore no children. She was marked severely by the pox that ravished her village, leaving her an orphan with failing eyes and a weakened body. Yet she stood defiant when asked to denounce her newfound religion and all that it brought to her people. Her miraculous survival of a two-month trek to escape her would-be killers and her ability to bring changes to a village in Canada have her memory well documented and preserved forever. Now, on the eve of her being canonized as a saint, her memory, life, and achievements have been brought to the forefront 350 years after she walked the narrow paths of her two villages. Kateri became sainted in October of the year 2012, and her story will be told over and over again for centuries to come.

Mohawk Chief

Chapter I
The Ancient Ones

I was Kenneronkwa, the war chief of the great Haudenosaunee Tribe, in life. My father before me was a great chief himself and was feared by all the nations even more than I am this day. I, too, have a son who will follow me at some point, and it is left to me to be his guide. I am looking for him now. I have left my earthly body to let it lie and rot in the mounds below us, and I can travel without it quite well. I hope it does feed my brothers from the underworld, whom I met there. It seems I have little use for it now and am glad to have been shed of its great weight. It has come to a good use, I feel, margins, and I have no ill will for what they do with it from here on—it was not for me to decide anyway. I travel free of them all on this new journey, yet I remember them so. I could not see them well, but they were ever present. It is not a place I soon will forget or want to ever return to.

Oh, how did this all come to be so? I was not prepared to leave my people without saying goodbye. It was not my time, was it? I miss only those of my own flesh, for I have been dead to them for many moons now, and they looked so sad. They have not come to meet me on this new trail even though I call out to them as they pass by, heading for their own journeys. I see them clearly through the forest and the low fog, yet they do not look to me. They just continue to travel their own ways. Why is it I cannot catch up to them before they are gone again? They seem to move as if they are in a dream world, I think. I do not know why this is so! Have I been outcast by the very spirits I prayed to over the countless fires? It was they who once walked the earth before me as well, was it not? They will not answer me when I call out to them regardless of how loud I become. I have beaten the empty water drum and tested a new flute, yet there is no response.

I stop occasionally as I walk this unknown path and yell to them over and over again as I wander along its rocky and well-trodden path. There is no answer at all from them as I remain here. They must step off the trail someplace and hide in the forest floor or high up in the trees as I pass. Why is it we never do meet? It would be great for them, because I have so much to tell them. Why are they doing this to me? Is this a new game they have learned that I don't know of? Are they possessed by the spirits of the netherworld? Why is it I do not know this? I have walked these many years alone without even the smallest brother beside me. I am truly no longer of their world—this is all I seem to know now. I must find a way to make things clearer to them, for I have so much to teach about our old ways. I fear, without me to guide them, all we have ever known will quickly be lost. I don't think you know enough to replace me, not yet anyway. There are no ancestors or elders or anyone at all with me this time, and it seems I am destined to continue on this lonesome trek without anyone's company beside me even on the coldest of nights.

I have called out to all of them, yet there have been no answers returning to my ears. The quick glimpses of them fade in and out as if they are walking in a strange darkness. I cannot track them when they leave no prints in the earth at all for me to seek. Not a blade of grass is disturbed, and even the wet dew is in its rightful place on the webs, unmolested. I do not understand this.

On the earth, I was a human being and the ruler of the great warriors of the Turtle Clan, but here I know little of them now, for they have ignored me so. Yet there are some things I will never forget, some things that come clearly to me. I must be in a great spell, for it is not what I was told it would be like here at all. We are the first of all humans to fall from the sky world and call the valley of the great river our home, are we not? Sky Woman created it all, and we were taught this all by our ancestors and the elders. They continue to send up the smoke from the great fire circles of the villages below to guide us, but are they listening to us anymore? To me, it does not appear so.

My beautiful wife, Kahenta, and my young son died with me, yet they refused to follow me to this place in the netherworld. It must be a struggle between the Creator and the divine woman, and she is only allowing me to follow her evil son, Tawis-karong of the left hand. She had no right, I say, but I allowed her to pray to her Jesus and Mary to keep peace in the longhouse. Is it now I am to be ruled by her ways and not mine? I will not allow this to be so. I am still the chief, am I not?

Is it Tijus-keha I must seek out, then? I think Kahenta must be following him instead of me. Is it Tawis-karong who will show me all the good there is to see in the light of a new sun? He is said to be the son of the right hand and easy to follow. Where do his tracks begin, I ask you? They are hidden too well. His younger brother is known to be a dweller of the darkness and sneaks from village to village with great monsters and terrible deceptions all around. He loved it so. I, for one, hope I do not meet him while I'm still here. Not that I would be afraid of him at all—I did not bring my club or lance with me. He is said to be a great warrior. But I think him a coward, for he has not shown himself yet. But there is still time.

Why am I so alone here? What evil did I conjure up in my old life that placed me here without the benefit of man, woman, or beast? There is plenty of room for you here as well and many more of us who no longer walk the earth! The darkness goes on forever, it seems, and my simple torch does not light much of anything that is ahead of me. I do not fear this dark place at all but need to light the way better just the same.

Where are all the elders and the people who came from the ancient villages who have gone long before me? They are the ones who taught us our ways! Do they go to a separate place where we cannot find them? Where are all the people of the great fire circles who told us the stories of our beginnings? I, for one, would enjoy a pipe now and again, and I was a good listener to their wild stories, wasn't I? Am I to remain in this place until the end of our time? Have I again been chosen to break the new trail, or will more follow me soon to share my chores? I have already built a new longhouse for them. It is a good and strong house of willow and bark, and it will hold many of her families as we did before. I have placed the sign of the turtle upon its openings for all to find. Yet I return to it often, and there is no sign that anyone has visited me except brother crow, and I must find the reason for this.

In life, I saw many a brave close his eyes for the last time as he fell in battle. Why aren't they here with me now? Didn't they die as well? There were so many children who were born still as the stone, yet they are not here. And what of those black robes who never cried out. None of them begged us to stop, not even once, as we tortured them to their deaths. Surely I am not alone here, yet all is silent. I can hear only the breath of me as it goes in and out. This, I remember too well, as it is a deafening sound. We have lost so many to the sickness of these men from the north, yet they do not carry the marks, do they? They hide their intentions so well in their long robes wrapped in the beads they have strung about them. They alone have brought about plague amongst us, and it has spread like the seeds of the meadow flowers upon wind. They have prayed against us, and our crops died in the sun from it. They are the evil, not us.

I, for one, cannot sleep in this place. I will torment the first of those who wear the black robes and come here aiming to rid us of our sacred rights. They came with their prayers hidden in the box of the gold metal packed full of evil thoughts and misdeeds. We stole it from their hands and threw it in our river. I saw it sink. I know it exists no more. It cannot harm us anymore, can it? Yet they still came into our villages to spread their disease with everything they carried in their sacks. They came praising their own god, telling us over and over again that our ancients and the Creator were of the left-handed son, Tawis-karong.

They tell us we are the doomed race, to be exiled to walk in this total darkness, and only they will be saved, not us. They do not know us at all, and yet they believe their god can save them from our flames. I, for one, do not believe anything will save them. They come with the green beads to entice our women and put a spell on the entire village. Oh, why is this so? They think we are weak like our cousins the Algonquins, or even the Hurons from the northland. I, for one, will show them we are not a timid group who act like frightened squaws, easily led their way. My warriors and I have roasted many of them as they were tied like dogs and kneeling before me. For I am Kenneronkwa, and I will not willingly give them our ancient homes. Least of all, I will not give up my people to their ways. I will make them all sorry they have disturbed me before it is done.

We have lost many of our villages to them, and I, for one, will not sleep in this place. I will seek out and torment these men of the black robes. I will do this to the end of all time. It will be the smoke of my fires they see, not the flames from their own destruction. Our camps and high castles that now light the night sky shall be revenged, I promise you this. They came with their words and idols, all so strange to us, and we took them in and fed them from our pots. We listened to them as if they were better than us and have forsaken our own traditions because they told us we must. Yet they came with the trade blankets and killed us by the house. Again, I watch them cautiously as they bow their heads while we bury our children under the mounds. Why is this so? They still come, first one at a time and then two or three of them traveling together much like a pack of coyotes. Sometimes I think they travel with our nations to the north to serve as their slaves.

I took their people, Father Jogues and the old one called Bressani. I gave them to the squaws to do woman's work. They will never again go to the fort to the north. They came under a flag of friendship yet wrapped the pox in the cloth they gave to us. It must have been woven into its very fabric, for we looked for it, but it could not be seen with our eyes. They, too, showed our men the flasks of wine and poisoned them as well. The wine set their heads to spinning like a child's toy, and none were ever the same men. I think they became more like the squaws or children. It must be very powerful. I, for one, need nothing from these people. I have everything I want just for the taking. Oh, I miss my life, and I have come to claim it again. My wife, my dear Kahenta, I miss the most, as she was young, a beautiful prize of war.

My daughter still walks among them, but she is barely alive, near blinded and marked because of their evil ways. Now she stumbles in her darkness without a word of sorrow or an unkind deed for any one of them. Why is this so? She is a chief's daughter, after all. My sweet infant son never had a real chance at life, and it is not fair. He was born a frail child and stayed upon the board for a long time, but he was loved so. He fell asleep as we all looked on and his life came out of him. I don't think he knew it. He was a peaceful child, no trouble to the women at all, but I would have made him a great and fierce warrior. He would have been respected as I am. I will haunt their houses and seek them out on the trail and follow them in our streams. I will not allow my people to die this way. It is they who bring this trickery to us, and it is they who will die in agony for all their trouble. We must remove these black robes from our forest before they gain a foothold and grow like the weeds after a harvest. There isn't room for both of us here. They kill everything in the name of their own Creator. Is he that powerful a chief, or is he just pure evil?

I will not allow my people to wonder how their children die before them. It should not be this way without it being of our own making.

We befriended them, and they killed us in return! Is this their type of mercy and divine goodness that they speak of so often? What makes them feel as though we should follow their ways and not those we have clung to for all times?

The elders of my youth told stories, around our fires, of the whites we befriended before these interlopers arrived. They were called the Dutchmen by them, but they were just a few. These were people who came through the woods only to trade for our pelts and took little else. They moved swiftly among us and vanished just as quickly. They told us of the English and of these Frenchmen, and they alone said we should keep an eye on their companions. They will sneak up and kill us dead for the land we have kept by our own fights. Yet they, too, traded us worthless goods, and we accepted them. Then they stole our squaws to keep them warm in the snow days. We did not mind this as much as we should have. When they told the elders of the signs the Frenchmen put on the trees, of the cross, it was an evil sign. It will bring sickness and much agony to this place, yet we laughed at them until it all came true. I forbade the children to make the sign even in jest. I, for one, do not want to upset our spirits. It was too late from that day on to prevent it.

Do all the whites wrap their disease in blankets and flasks? Why do they prey on their own kind? Is their world so terrible they must find shelter here? I have heard this is so. I trust not one of these men who slither like the snake, and we are well advised to stay away from them as much as we can. We do not need them for anything, for we can provide for ourselves. We have shared our stores with them when they were in need. It is not the other way as they tell their kind. Many have been found frozen to the earth, for they come in the contempt of the winter. As foolish as that is, they do not learn from it. They travel all the seasons to reach us. We must always be on the lookout. I will not show them any quarter when we meet again, as I did to them on Mother Earth and now regret it. I will always be on this side of the victory when it comes to a fight, but I prefer to just avoid them now. They are not worthy of a Mohawk lance, or a blow from a well-swung club, unless they attack us first. They will see all our teeth at once.

Oh, I miss my life and have come to claim it again. I miss my wife the most, as she was mine to keep. I have no other worries than to find them again, and I will seek the council of the great spirits to teach me what I must know to be with her again. I will not allow them to keep me away. I will find my braves holding their pikes and drive out all those who insist on cheating me of life. Have I started this terrible journey alone, without family? I will look for them until I cannot travel anymore. It is not of my resolve to be kept here without knowing about them.

Those of the Jesuits came to us praising their gods. They were led to our villages by those whites we allowed to come to fish and trap in our valley. We traded with them. They even enjoyed our pipes and took much of the leaf when they left. They lived among us for a time and even took our squaws as theirs in the ceremonies, same as us. Yet they come now to take our very being, for we are in their way to the great ponds and forests still walked by the deer, elk, and beaver. We are doomed to die a death with no sky and no ocean. I believe that would be a horrible place for us. I have found such a place as I journey back to a village I have seen in this world, and I, for one, am not satisfied to be here.

They must be driven from this place forever. I must continue to seek a way to find my own village again. I will rid the earth of them when I get there and will kill all those who follow their ways of the cross and beads. They talked of the old times and the ancients as if they knew them as we do. They talked of their Creator and his mother as if it was the true beginning, yet they know nothing of our Sky Woman. They talked of the darkness and the loneliness of their places. They pray on their knees, holding their beads. They talk of the great powers they possess, yet I am not afraid of them. I do not see their weapons as any mightier than ours, and I know my braves are stronger and will not flinch as they do. I wish them a peace that can only come at the end of an arrow or even a shot.

They must lead the way for us to follow, as we are comfortable without their knowledge of such destinations and their people. We, after all, have been here since the beginning of time, haven't we? What could they possibly teach us? They must be gone from here! They came with their green beads and wooden crosses. They used them and their boxes of spells to place a curse upon our heads. Then, when we did not allow them to take our spirits, they placed this curse upon all who walk beneath the sign of the Mohawk. Why was this so?

We meant them no harm. We shared our food and our forest with them until they took too much from us. It was our women and children who fell to their evil ways first, not I who was fooled by the outstretched hands and toothy smiles of them holding back that evil tongue. They brought my people the gifts of bead and cloth, and now can you see what we got for the trouble? It was they who wrapped their disease in the blankets of the colors we began to know— those same blankets with the stripes of yellow, green, and red we had been offered as gifts from them now so many times. Oh, they tricked some with all of this, and it is they who now must pay for it. The flasks of the fermented wine spoiled our sons as well as the many who died from its impure excess.

Oh, I miss my life and have come to claim it again, as I was not ready to die. I hear my infant son as he coos in his deep sleep. I, for one, cannot find him yet, but there is time.

The earth voyage, I now leave to my brother, as he became the new chief. He is a good man yet weaker in many ways than I. I taught him all he needs to know, and maybe he will grow to learn more of life on his own. I haven't the time to spend with him now, and he is relishing in his new place. I can see that from here. He must learn to turn them away from the village and keep them at bay. It falls to him to punish them and, if necessary, to stake them to the lodgepoles in shame. He means no harm to anyone who did not kill us.

We war with the Algonquins and some of the Hurons, but they aren't worth our best. We take them to work our fields and gather wood for our women. They seem to enjoy this, for they always decide to stay when we send them home again. We take their squaws to our lodges, and they, too, wish to stay when we tell them they may leave us. They are good women and bear us many children. Some we let feed the earth, but they did not follow me here, as I am still alone.

We have fought our enemies with all our might, and we have always stayed the victor in the end. Sometimes even when we meet them on the trails, we give them little or no quarter. Their young bucks will try to reclaim the path, but they will fall where they stand, for we are not a tribe to be reckoned with. We will let them pass with unbent heads, but if they show the sign of arrogance, we will surely put them to death. They, too, have suffered from the black robes' sickness, and their losses are as great as ours, yet they continue to trade with these worthless dogs. I will not allow them in my camp when I return. We will repel them before they see the village gate. Only the crows flying on wing will know they were here, for soon there will be nothing left to tell their story.

Oh, my children, I miss you so. Where have you gotten to? I can feel you near me, yet you are not in sight. Why is this so? I walk the trails, looking for you to come greet me, yet you do not show yourselves to me. Are you hiding from me? I follow the voices of our people, looking for the glow of your fire in the darkness, but there is no light coming from it. You do not look for me, and I do not understand this. I see my mother, and she beckons me to follow her, but I must refuse, for I do not want to remain here as she did. I have seen my father too. He doesn't look well. He has long since been dead, I'm afraid, and he no longer can hear me when I call out to him. He does have his pipe, as he sits by a warm fire most of the time. That is a good place for him. I think he does have others to talk to, but I cannot find a way to reach out to him and let him know I'm here. But I will, and they will never forget when that happens.

I expect you to answer me, but you do not. Can you hear me as I call out into this darkness? I would expect you to step up and greet me as you did in life. But you have not. Oh, I long for those days with us in the longhouse of your grandmother. She, too, should be here, but she is not. Do not be afraid if I appear to you, for I come to protect you and keep you from harm once again. I will stand over you as you sleep, and no one will disturb you. Oh, I miss all of this so!

I have followed the trail to the Dutch land and beyond. I have forded the many streams and rivers between here and there, and crossed the great one to the north without getting wet. I have ascended the hills with the ease of a young buck, but no one has come along to speak with me or show me the final way to reach you. I so wish you would just look up from your own slumber and reach out to me. It would end all of my misery. Why is it you cannot understand me? I have visited the fishing grounds, but there is no one there. Have they all found other places to set up their wears?

I see some young braves in the valley, and they make sport of the priest of the black robes they have surrounded. He will not be killed this day but end up as a prize for some squaw before he receives his reward in the end of it. They will make him naked and crawl for their mercy before they strip his flesh. He will then be treated the way of all cowards, and he will bear the marks of the blades from head to foot before they end his miserable life and clean the flesh from his bones. He will sit in the fire ring to brighten the night sky for us. I have met Chief Kiotsaeton and his own white man, Couture. They again have arrived at our three rivers, and we again will sit in council, speaking of war again. That will be a good time. I fear Kiotsaeton has lost his nerve though. Maybe they have used their evil spells from the gold box on him as well and his mind is gone. I fear he, too, will go to the bent knee of the black robes and say the prayers that they demand. Our small council does not resolve them of my death but only fortifies my death and their lies. They claim to come in peace, yet many of us die at their hand just the same. They are not to be trusted.

They speak of their Creator like he is above us all. I, for one, feel he doesn't exist. We already have a Creator, and there is no need for two of them—that, I am sure of. The weakness of the Hurons and their kin the Algonquins shows me I am right. Our Creator must have a sense of humor. The black robes have made them all like their squaws. They pretend to honor our ways and set great feast before us around the fires when we visit with them. Yet they are not our friends—even the good Father Lamberville, whom we do trust a little, for he does not fear us. He says it is all just a dream that we see. He refuses to listen to our people's tales and calls us liars. Yet he has done as I wish and does not preach to those who turn him away from their lodges. This is all I ask of them. I, for one, do not believe this man at all. He can show me no proof of his idle claims.

We will go build a new castle, only to have them sneak up on our children as they lie on the rugs and kill them as they sleep. They again will set it all to the torch until there is nothing but some char where their houses once stood. I will give them no more presents in their councils. I have given my only son and my good wife to their cause. Isn't that enough? I have died so they can prosper from our riches of pelt and fish. Our crops lie trampled under their feet as they walk aimlessly through our forest, looking for the last of us. Oh, I wish to return to my human form, for I will seek to torture each of them over again at least one hundred times, for they are worthless compared to us. I will return those who have walked to the beyond at their hand and help them find their way to our villages again. I can almost hear the laughter of the children running through the yards and tugging at our tents.

Kahenta, oh, how I have missed you so since we last met. Why is it that I cannot sense you near me? Do you have the hand of our son tightly in your grip, or is he still strapped to the board in the soft fur of the rabbit? I left you in the longhouse so I could run ahead and make it all safe for you. But it seems you did not follow me to this place. Why is this so? I cannot hear your soft voice, nor feel the warmth of your skin next to me. I am being punished by the spirits of our ancestors, and I know not why. The Creator must not have liked my worldly deeds as much as I did in carrying them out. I, for one, would not change anything I have done in my earthly body. It cannot be so.

I have led my warriors in the attacks to the east, and I raised my goblet to the victory feasts so many times, their blood still thick upon my hands. I suspect these men of the black robes for every ill that has befallen us. No one has told me I am not right. They came with the broad smile of a friend, carrying that cursed box of mischievous demons within, disguised as if it were a new child's toy. The caw of brother crow shows me the way to go, so I shall hunt for you all, as he is my only true guide. I cannot rely on you anymore to do it for me. I grow impatient.

They all claim to be men of a god and only come in peace. Yet they left in deceit and caused many of us to die—a dreadful death of sores and a haunting cough that stole our breath in the middle of the night when all those of trickery are about. They claim to come in peace yet steal our pelts for the price of a few glass marbles or beads. They pile them high upon the ass, almost breaking its back. Why is this so? I, for one, feel their Creator doesn't exist, for we already have our own, and there just is no need for two. Our men will slay them all every time we see them, and they will be run down easily if they are on foot. We have slain them all before this time when the wars were to our favor. We will continue to do so in this quiet time as well. When the day arrives that they come no more, we will all be happy again. That is something I would surely like to see. We know our Creator, and he has served us well. He will not let us down now if we ask for his help. I know this from my own teachings from my father, and the elders have told me this so many times before this day as well.

The weakness of the Hurons and their kin, the lowly Algonquins, shows me I am right. They have gone to the knee and refuse to fight us anymore. It is these Frenchmen with their colors of red and blue that we must keep an eye upon. They seem to multiply like the hares we teach our children to trap with the snare. We have been pushed away from the great rivers and huddled into smaller camps in winter to protect us from them.

Yet we go on and build a new castle in the spring of the seasons only after leaving the old one in flames. We will sing and drink to its skyward send. But these men are the sneaks of the night and come here without our wishes and slay our children where they lie on the rugs. I do not trust them at all and respect them even less. I have already given them my own son. Isn't that enough for them? Many have done the same as we have. We are fewer now and will have a hard winter. Yet they still come to our gate over and over again, asking for handouts like a begging dog! Sometimes they bring with them men with the long guns, and we scatter for a time into the forest. We have been betrayed by these cowards too many times to trust them again. We will all come together on the fields once again to drive them from here. I want to end this once and for all. It will just take some time for our children to learn our ways and fear nothing but that of defeat itself. When they are ready, I will again lead them—that, I promise you.

My wife is gone forever, as I am, yet they still come in close to us and steal our crops under the cover of the night like the foul dogs they are. She would spend her days in the fields pulling all the weeds and toting the water on the dry days. Now her plot is overgrown, with nothing left except the hummingbirds flickering from leaf to leaf without ever landing. I have no time to watch their dance—there isn't time for such things anymore. The tormentors still come from behind the trees and the shelter of the great rocks to see if she has grown more corn, and when they find nothing left there for them to steal, will this all end? They grow so little of what they need, and taking ours has become their way. They are unfit for the pot, and we do not fear the man, but it is their deeds we mistrust. Oh, I will seek out the Creator, for he is all I have left. He must give me a sign to follow. He rules over all the natives whether they are in the federation or not. He has not walked with me for a long time now. I must listen for him, as he must be near.

We have seized the Jesuits' box and tossed it into the river to drown its evil inhabitants. Yet our crops continue to fail as the water turns brown and then green. The land has little left to bring to the surface except the occasional mole.

The priest they called the good Father Jogues died by the hatchet for his deception to us. His heavy head was lofted upon a thick pole at the edge of our village to warn his entire ilk they were not welcome here. I don't think it has silenced him though. Not even for all of their worthless presents can they walk here unmolested. They can come to us carrying many goods they feel we will take, but I, for one, need nothing from them. I have everything we need right under my feet. They come with the sacks full of these goods to try to make us change our ways. No more of these cowardly men they call the black robes will be able enter our walls unless they are bound and led in by the children. They will not fare well for theory killings of our Mohawks, I promise you this.

Our scouts continue to see them running away from us and hiding deeper in the forest to try to escape. Escape, they cannot. I, for one, hope it will not be long before we give them the fear that will drive them from the deepness of these woods forever. I will gladly put them all to a horrible death should we catch them. I will make it a long and painful time for them, for they do not heed our warnings now and keep coming more and more each day. I doubt we will change our ways to be on bent knees by the Jesuits and go to their altar in prayer. I, for one, do not see the end of these battles until all of them are killed or have fled like children, running until they drop still along the path. Then we will let the dogs feast upon the carcasses, and finally we will feed the earth again with them. They do not grow good corn though.

I have been told by my brother that they are many more than us and that more still remain hidden form us behind the great sea. I hope he is mistaken. Even if we count all our enemies as one great nation, they still have more villages to gather their men from than we do, or so I am told. They seem to come as if a plague or a brush fire is driving them forward and they are running away from it. They don't seem to fear our lances like they should once we find them in our woods, for it seems what they have left behind is deadlier than even we are to them. Is there such a tribe that we the Iroquois cannot tame? Have we met our end of our time here already? The ancestors have told us of such a time, but it cannot be this soon, can it? What of our people? What will become of them? Are they to become nomads again, scratching at the earth for food as we did in the beginning? Are we to hide in the mountain caves again, where they are dripping with the winter snows? It has not come to pass, has it?

Even the thought of us living alongside them in a quiet peace is still enough for them to seek out a new way on the path when we meet. They are the ones who came into our world to disturb us, yet is it us they do not trust? We have done nothing to make them feel this way, and I, for one, believe they are all evil and cannot be changed—I even feel that for those of them who have been whelped here. We have been treated like children by them, and I, for one, will not let that stand. I am a great chief, a warrior, and it is my place to send them away.

First they send their scouts with their black robes following behind, all snug in their wool vestments secured by their shiny crosses. Then they creep yet a little closer and send us the trade goods and then steal our thick pelts. Then they bring the long guns to battle our club and axe until we have so few we cannot resist. This cannot be what the elders have seen for our people, can it? I must assemble them again as soon as I return. I will build a great fire and draw them from all of our villages. We must resist them all, for they wish us no good, I feel. I don't think they are human beings. I know not what some of my people see in them, and there must be some magic about if we have allowed a few to remain in our camps, and some others have become brothers.

Still some take our women as theirs and are welcomed by them. Their children are not as strong as ours at birth. Some will fight our enemy with us, and some seem touched. They had told me that I, too, must look at the future, but my vision only sees them as enemies, not as we see the Hurons or even the Algonquins, for they at least can tend our fields once we capture them. These people smell of the skunk to me and are not welcome in my lodge.

I can raise all confederacies against them, I am sure of this. My brother tells us there are more of them than all the sand on our shore. I, for one, don't think my brother knows much. I have traveled to the north region through the thick woods and beyond the great rivers where they have come from, and they remain there as well. They build their castles of stone and mud, and they do not bend the willow as we do. They clear all the trees from their lands so we cannot sneak up on their camps. They do not let us challenge them. We must learn all their ways so we can defeat them, for they are a strong enemy in more than just numbers, it seems. They have the evil magic and come to us with offerings that seem hard for us to resist, yet we have been here for a thousand years and have not needed them all this time. Our spirits have grown silent to us when they are near. It is not said what we must do, so for now, I will watch them from here, where they cannot see me. It is my brother I have left behind to protect my village. I feel he will need all the other chiefs' guidance to overcome these intruders. I, for one, am not always sure he pays attention to us.

I can see neither my wife nor my son! But I can see you, my dear. Oh, how you have grown from that little child, and now you look like your mother did when I last saw her. You almost fooled me. You glow, my dear child, as I look down upon you. I see all the children huddling in close to you, waiting to hear you say the prayers you have been taught by them that I now must seek out. I can hear your kindness. I can sense your loving touch. I see you passing from tent to tent and pausing at the longhouses that have the sick. It is you who is not afraid of them or any thought of yourself. I, for one, would stay away.

My dear Tekakwitha, I miss you so much it is hard not to hold you near. But I can see you almost as If I were there, for you come to me in my dreams, I think. I long for our walks beside the great river and to hear your laughter melting the cold nights. I long for your smile as you look up into my face. Most of all, I long for your comforting voice. I long to see us all together again and need to ask your help in finding the rest. I long for you to take your brother's hand and teach him to run. I long for the days that have sped past without even a thought of us to come back to me. I fear, Tekakwitha, that you, my daughter, must continue alone on this journey. It was not my choice to leave. You have learned their ways the most of all of our people and know how they think.

Oh, I wish we could talk again by the light of the cook fire. There is so much for me to know. You seem to know their god as well as you know our Creator. I heard you speaking to him many times when I was there, walking the same paths as you. And it is you who thinks their god is the same as our Creator, yet I have not been convinced this is true. You talk of his mother as if she were beside you. Can she be as sweet as you say? I, for one, have chosen the path of our ancestors, for it is the only one I know, but as your story will be told one hundred moons from now, you will be remembered for all the good deeds you do. I love you, my little Tekakwitha, and I miss you the most, but it isn't me you call for in the darkness—it is him. This, I do not understand. Why is this so? We will all sit one day at the great council circle, and I, for one, want to meet him. It will be up to me to decide if he is a friend or enemy, not you, my child, for it is my right as chief to welcome them into our camp.

You must walk among them for some time to come. Learn all their ways well. Learn the ways of the brothers and the sisters and the fathers, and of the man they call "Lord." I cannot be with them from where I am at this moment, but I will find a way. Is he truly our Creator that you pray to, or is he some mystic they have made holy? Will he be truly bringing all his people to the beginning as they claim, or will it all end in a mound of this earth?

The only thing I ask of you, my dear sweet child, is to hurry along your own path, for I and your mother wait for you. Brother has his outstretched hand waiting for your touch again. Let him walk beside you, and guide him when you can. Our journey is done, I fear, and I have not found the path back to you yet. I will continue looking until we meet again.

You must, for now, start at the beginning and tell all who will listen of your family and villages, for there is no one left to tell our story. We have walked this earth for more than a thousand years. With these interlopers here, it may come to an end oh too soon. I don't think our people will live another one hundred years more. It is a short time, I fear. They came of only one purpose, and that is to take all they can and leave us with nothing. They came to take all that is ours and replace it with theirs. I have seen both sides now, and I fear for the worse. When I look upon you, I see all the hope for us because of this, and all in our world is bright again. The future of us, while less than clear, has a bright light, and it is you. I, for one, don't feel we should give up our lands to them, yet they come and strip it of our trees, foul our water, and turn up great patches of our earth, only to leave it bare the next season and move on to another. We are in their way, and they have set the goal of removing us from here. I, for one, will again walk the earth and resist.

Oh, my daughter, I try to reach out to you, and I know you can feel me near. I have seen what they have done to you, and I will come visit them another time when they are sleeping. I will cause them to come to this place and free me from its bonds. Oh, my daughter, you were born of a great family and a loving mother, who held you high into the night sky and said the words of the Jesuits over you. Never did you cry or gain the sickness until we all almost left this earthly place. You, my dear, were the only one to escape this death that holds on to me and has set me on this journey to regain my life. No one should have to endure the trials that have followed your life. I, as a chief, know what is expected of the men in battle, but for you to endure these daily assaults shames me so.

You, my daughter, are such a sweet child. They will pay for the false words and stones they throw at you. I look down from this sky place and know we will be together soon. I see you raise your eyes toward me—can't you see me beyond the clouds? Oh, my daughter, you spend your days in such a peaceful state. I notice this most. Your heart is full, and your words are to their god, yet it is all right with me. I see that you have richness in your life that I, as your father, could only hope for you to receive. You, my daughter, are without a man, yet you have all you will ever need. I see from my perch that you will accept the toil they lay at your door. You school the children, raise the corn, and make the gowns for others to wed in. Yet you are a happy child, and no one will see you cry.

You, my daughter, are a chosen one. It is plain for me to see. Our gods have spoken to me, and they say you will become holy to them. I, for one, wish to be with you, but there is little that you need. I have shaken the tree above you many times for you to notice me. I have seen your face as it glows in the light of a new day. You do not want for anything, yet you seek their lord. I have no sight of your mother, but that journey has not ended as well. I know she taught you her ways. I turned my eyes to others so she could get you to understand. You have her beauty and all of her special traits. It will be up to you alone to spread the words of her people among all those who come near. And, my darling little daughter, as you grow and become a woman, I want you to know I will always be with you, always seeking out your wisdom. I know you are in a special peace the rest of us may never know.

My hope for you is that you look up toward me as I remain locked in this place and say the words that will bring us all—Mother, Brother, and yes, me—to your earthly place once again. I will wait here, my child, but don't ask me to be patient, for I miss you so. I know you will honor us who have gone before you. But be not in such a hurry to join us in this place, for you are greater than even I, Kenneronkwa, the great war chief. You have chosen an unblazed path for yourself, and it will be twisted and run deep into the woods. But you, my dear, are well equipped to see your way to the place you know must be around the next bend, for in your sightless world, you can see everything you need. So for now, my precious daughter, I will continue to watch from the sky. It is up to you to find out how we will meet again. When it will happen, I do not know, and why all this has happened to us, maybe your new god can tell us.

Farewell, my daughter. I leave it all to you. Our fate will be in your hands from this day on. I look at you in wonderment, for you are so small and weak, yet there is no one else who can keep us alive. Look to the sky, my dear child, and I will step out from behind a big cloud to give you direction when you ask for it. I must go forward now and seek your mother and her child. When we catch up to them, I will make sure we wait for you to join us when your work is done. I will save you a nice place beside me around our newly lit fire. If you wish to live among them for a while longer, it is all good with me. I must go now, for I can hear them calling but cannot find the right path to greet them yet. I will talk to you again soon, I hope. Tell your uncle I spoke with you, and give him some guidance if you can. He is the stubborn one, and he might not listen.

Hunting Village Preparing a Meal

Chapter II
Blood in the Snow

The harshness of this winter has worn heavily on us, all of the tribes of the Algonquin and Iroquois Nations. We are enemies, yes, but still, after all, brothers of the seasons. We give and take so much from each other. They always give more in their peaceful ways than we do in ours, and we show little in the way of mercy upon them as we take their lands for our own, their people for our servants, and their squaws for our women. Those who resist will lie dead and still until the next snow covers them where they fall, and all is clean and fresh again for now.

Many of our villagers have not survived in our human form when the snows of the north came so early this season, covering our longhouses well above that of any year since the great ice. Many now bow under its great weight, yet we still remain within them to seek the warmth of the fires tended by the maidens so young and peaceful. We have been told of this ancient time so many years ago by our elders, who have taught us our ways and see the visions from the great fire rings of our own people who have passed on to them our future in the spirit world. Those stories keep their spirits alive, and the fires that were built once long ago to see them have finally burned out as well. They now lie cold and still without any signs of life among their embers, no sounds of the snow hissing as it touches the ground or stones around them. No puddles for the dogs are there, nor is there warmth from its glow. Yet there is still life in the ashes we have now lifted to the sky on the winter winds, and we watch them falling to earth and blackening the path for us to clearly see our way. If only we choose to follow them and those who came before us. We can only remember their faces in the songs of the drum and flutes. Those around this circle will not be forgetting the bite this still night air has placed on us. We will sing and chant their praise as all are now remembered.

Many others will come to life only in songs of the shaman, and we hear the drone of their drum circles from here to the great waters. Each and every day, we will continue to seek their wisdom and guidance, for they are many. We have made the attempt to bring our brothers to us and make them our family, and many do stay as our children, for we have made them orphans. Yet both camps are again warring, and within our own ranks, we see little to tell us we will not be the victors. We see them in the trees and behind the great stones, or running the rivers as the snow melts, always trying to gain advantage of us. We must always be wary of the calls and silence of a night like this.

Attacks are common now, and they, too, have the men of the flesh coming with them. Those men of the black robes follow along with them from camp to camp, their guards and warriors well concealed behind those high-walled villages of tall timber and stone that they escape to as we draw near. But it wasn't always so. These intruders have bribed us both with coin and spirits, and we have forsaken our own heritage in the promise of a better way of life, one they claim is eternal—something we already believe we have obtained over and over again.

We are forced to a bent knee to honor their god and serve their elusive kings or be damned for it until it all ceases to be. They wish to punish us for keeping to our own ways, yet many of their ways are peculiar and leave everything in their path dead or dying for nothing more than sport, it seems. But we are what they call the savages and the ones who need to find redemption? They have befriended us and taken many of our pelts, bedded our squaws, and demeaned everything we hold dear. But what is the price? Maybe we receive a few pieces of glass or a trade blanket with its colors of red and green or yellow. Or perhaps if we are lucky, a new hatchet or maybe a clay pipe will be handed to us for a long winter's toil?

The iron trinkets they have often given us in trade, we have now pounded into blade and sharpened upon the hard stones of the earth. Others still will adorn our necks as tokens of knowing them. The weapons and the supplies they drop in battle, we will pick up and carry with us back to our lodges. Only then will we make more spears and pikes from them, for we intend to drive them all back across the great waters, and the sooner we do, the better we will all be. I, for one, see no equality in this relationship.

They wish themselves upon us, and I, for one, will refuse their god and them as well. To me, they are nothing more than mere men who need many to protect themselves better from us. Where we can run away from their musket and ball, they cannot follow us without fear we will spring upon them and remove their spirits from their chests. They will lose their way without us, and then they, too, become ours or fall flat faced in their tracks, starving amongst the plenty; and then they, too, become easy prey to the animals that walk the night around them, ever searching.

I, for one, will hang the head of their Charles on my lodgepole if he should ever come here to claim his own share of what is not intended for him to possess. I find him a coward, for he sends these puny men with the odor of the caves to wrestle away what we have died repeatedly to obtain—then to squander it all away again or let it spoil on the ground where it lies. He seems content for now to send these inferior beings to us, however. If they take root like the weeds of the fields, they will overcome us, and we will be lost forever. It will not be long, I fear, that we must wait for him and his red jackets to show up, lining the banks across from us, and then we must fight not only those of the north, but we will now have to look to the east as well.

I am told from those we capture and torture, they will come in droves like locusts to drive us from this place. We have seen them with their strange, selfish ways, and we have heard their cannon that trails behind their beasts and their villages that spring up like the popal of the forest that are built on our scared grounds, where our ancestors once stood vigil. We will not allow them their final wishes, not today or anytime soon.

We of the Mohawk are to be feared and respected. It is our brothers, the Algonquins, we raid to plow our fields. We will not fear them, but we will put fear into them. And their scalps will hang in honor on the pikes in front of our lodges for all who wander by to see and admire. The black robes must know we do not welcome them, for they are the same as those who come to do us harm. They come here with their strung beads and thick book, hiding under the brim of the wide hat, only wishing to change our children and turn them against us. I will not stand alone against them, for we will fight to our last for our ways, and our ancestors are with us to guide us on this path until we are no more.

The French come from the wide river far above those and us they call the English, coming from the great shore where the sun comes out of the sea early each new day. It is they who continue to put pressure on all our rights to hunt and trap along the newly discovered lands west of the place and disturb our other tribes of the nation we once called Shawmut, all the way to the great waters that run wide and deep, and to our brethren of the Chickasaw or the Miami people. Those tribes and their clans around us now and our brethren to the east and west have held this ground against all odds for centuries—now without much more than a minor skirmish to hold fast to it, for they have come to take all they touch from us.

We want nothing more than our rights to live, hunt, and fish without their influences. Before even the Clan of the

Bear or the Tribes of the Turtle lived here, our ancestors and gods were here, and they shared this place with all who cared to forage or chase the deer throughout the forested uplands as well as across the sweetgrasses closer to the river's edges. Now they, too, are driven away by those who come and take only the pelt, watching the meat rot under the very sky we worship. Yet they claim divinity above us. We roamed over this land and protected each animal, the birds circling above us, each and every tree, the green blades of grass, and even the smallest insect under our feet from squander or invasion—for this is our homeland, not theirs.

We have not been alone for some time now. First they came as a dribble and then like a perennial stream, but now the great beaver has removed his dam and the flood is a human one, not of the liquor of life. It is the men of those from the great ships who have brought with them their peculiar ways of the parchment and quill, proving it is indeed their land, not ours. They bring their sickness and weeping wounds wrapped all in the trade.

The English come here with their matter-of-fact feeling of divine ownership. They claim all that surrounds them and declare it theirs in the name of their King Charles, their own Sun King. He, for one, has not yet set foot on our soil, and we know not of his place, but if he rules there as these men who wander the woods tell us, he will not live long. The French come with their beads strung loosely around their middle, and they wear nothing but the finery of their great village of Paris, under the vestments so fashioned to keep the cold of this winter and the warmth of our summer from ever reaching their nakedness.

Their King Louis isn't likely to come here, I'm told by those we have captured, as he has troubles enough of his own in his village. Yet he continues to send these black robes here with their own ways and beliefs. But they come here still, with their wanting to change us and make us mimic them and forsake our own ancestors for theirs. Yet they are little good at serving us, and I, for one, feel they all pray to their Creator, and I, for one, wish to send them all there to meet him, the sooner the better.

I come alone from the great waters to the easterly of this place, but I, too, am welcomed and brought into the huts and sleep among them and eat at their fire rings within their lodges. The great water below us does not cover herself with the thick of ice and snow in winter yet stays open and allows us to portage a great distance in search of the now-sparse deer or caribou of our brothers to the northern villages. When we meet them on the trails and they demand we step aside to allow them clear passage, I, for one, will not break a stride to allow them that privilege. I am the son of a chief long since on his own journey to meet the Creator, and I, too, take his place as head of this clan. I bring my brother's child with me, as do my sisters, for who among us would bring this child into their lodge or village without the benefit of sight or strong back to do the woman's work and carry the water.

For I am Iowerano, the chief of the Mohawks and brother of Tsaniton-gowa, who was in life the great war chief of all the Turtle Clan. To honor his memory, I will watch over this dear child as if she were my own. I will bring her to our new village and raise her as a Mohawk woman, and she will be safe from all harm among her people. Here, I will make her forget the ways of the black robes and her mother.

I will not allow anyone to drive us from this place, for all of my race will stand up one day together and take bow and spear up against them all if it comes to us that we fear we are near the end of our time. It is, after all, our sacred land. Our fathers told us to stay, and our ancestors rise up from the council smoke of our fires and guide us through these difficult times. We are the natives who were here when the bridge ceased to exist, the tribes who watched the moon as it has grown cooler to our eyes ever since we have been here. We did not inherit this land—we were born from it. But we are now at the mercy of our alliance, an uneasy one at best. We have been promised much from these French, with their peculiar language and dress. Some wear the long black robes of their priest and clergy, and some they call "father" and others merely "brother," but we must obey them and be laid prostrate in front of them. Whether it is the skin of a long-dead bear or elk, or the bright-white snow that has fallen cold and pure and covers us, it matters not to them.

To them, we are their children and must obey their every command or perish from this place stained now and forever red with the blood of our kin and haunted by the screams of our adversaries.

My brother was chief of the Mohawks and leader of the Turtle Clan. Kahenta was his squaw and mother to a small, sickly child known only as "Tekakwitha," although the missionaries of the black robes call her differently—and I protest this often and aloud. It wasn't for her mother to call her this. It is a Christian name, and as she prays the way of these whites with their superior airs and customs, I, for one, shall not allow this to be. I, as chief, deny the god of their king and refuse his word to be spoken under the tents and skins of my lodges and longhouse. I will cast them out into the cold night of the quiet death and watch them become still before I will acknowledge the ways of these men who come with a book and a heavy hand. They come here not to bend us like the tall pine in the wind but to snap us like the brittle twigs of the alder.

It almost all has long since been forgotten except by our shaman and a few elders still willing to speak of it. She came from the village of her dead parents, where her brother was bound to his mother's still chest. All she knew as a child, she has remembered, and she feels she knows enough to keep their memory alive without our assistance. They are interned therein on the mound to stop the sickness that scars her to this day. They were the lucky people, for their death ended their horrid and painful journey.

No more is the village they named Ossernenon visible on the banks of the river. It has all but been hidden by Mother Earth and her children of cedar and pine. Today we are at Caughnawaga, my new village of the brave and the strong. It is all a wonderful place befitting of my station. We are preparing to move there soon enough, but our final destination, like the white elk, still eludes us all, for now.

Tomorrow we will speak to the elders around our fires and smoke and feast with them to find our way again. It is they who, through talking with the Great Spirit, find the best ways to protect us. We are here but a short interlude to find our strengths and pick our best for the events that will test us all. The braves we shall choose will go into the next battle aware of their odds yet alive with the spirits of those who walked this ground before us all within their chests. My family is growing again, yet our longhouses are small, and we will not have the great space as before. But we need to be drawn nearer to each other to teach and protect one another.

They come out of the forest at night to begin burning our longhouses and all the forest between our small and scattered settlements. They are killing the earth for all of us, as little will sprout on the desolated floor where the great pines once stood. It is a wasteland, and they will not survive as a people for long if they continue to plunder all the Great Spirit's creations. His songs are sad, and his ravens will tell the story over and over again as they push deeper and deeper into the trees to escape the sight of them. We hear them in murder and alone. Their wings weigh heavily as they pass over our camps and trails, never seeming to touch down but constantly circling on the winds. The drums rattle slowly, with quiet strength, not the beating that arouses the hearts of his people. No, today we prepare to raise an axe and spear and watch the women as they shed their tears for us, for they know we will not all return from our quest. But death of this earthly body isn't the final order. It is only the beginning.

The brightness of this night's sky tells us it will be soon that we raid across the river. No persons of their village will survive us if we have the elders and spirits of our ancestors awakened within us. They shall become alive again to protect us and guide us through this darkness. We must sit in war council and praise those who have walked before us, for now we will meet them in the middle of the great stream, and they, too, will be victorious with us in scraping these imposters from our lands once and for all.

The children of our village run amuck in and out of the white stones carefully placed to keep the embers from falling on our robes. Yet we barely notice their actions. They have chased the dogs and beaten the drums in their constant passing, tripping over nearly every gourd set upon the earth for us to drink from. They send them rolling hither and thar, in all directions throughout the circle, adding to their amusement before the squaws come and fetch them for wash and their cot. We are a fortunate clan of Mohawks, for it is the children of this village who will see us through these hard times and comfort us with their laughter and antics in the lodges when those of us who remain grow white like the snow itself.

But we must get through today alive, and as we rise from the earth like the smoke swirling and jumping upward as it carries the embers like fireflies into the heavens, we are young again as well. The youngest of our men have all at the ready. We must not let them stray too far out in front of us, for they will give our intentions away before we can reach their camp on the far side of our woods. I will remember this day always as I look back one last time toward my village and the child Tekakwitha, with her blind eyes searching the sky and her lips pursed as she speaks out into the blackness, for she was born of the Christian woman of the Algonquins and my brother, who was my chief first before they all went to stay with our ancestors. The boy never reached an age of anything that mattered much, but there was promise in his bright eyes and shining face—that was, of course, before the sickness brought by the black robes killed them all. They are a strange lot, I think.

She remained there as the last great canoa was skillfully lifted from its resting place, hidden no more amongst the trees, and quietly set upon the waters as if it were a fragile leaf. We are gone now, but we shall return soon, and she will be waiting for us as she always is, for she is patient with all around us, and even the animals that hide from us know she has no hatred or fire in her bosom and come out from under the scrub to be nearer to her. She prays with her sister, Anastasia, for what we undertake this day. She alone can say the words of the black robes, as I have forbidden it to be heard on the winds by anyone else. She does not disobey me, but I think she cannot hear me well.

But it will be a day of sorrow for both villages, and many a lodgepole will run red and black tonight, for we have engaged them, and they, too, were prepared by summonsing their ancestors to guide them. The battle is swift, and many fall where they stood, defiant and tense. Yet they fought bravely, and in the falling light, many appear as if they have lain down to sleep. Those who will survive this day will be tied and dragged to their feet to march back with us, reluctant at best. We all will carry our dead back across the streams to bury in their ancestral mounds with a little food and their hawk to accompany them for their journey. Perhaps the clay marbles will accompany them as well. I'm sure some are not finished with their game earlier in this day. As many as thirty of our best canoas pushed silently away in the early morning, cloaked still in darkness, with only seventeen to return. We will come for them another day, once the stench of this place has been swallowed by Mother Earth or the bones have met the mice.

The gods of those looking down upon our battle favored them this day, not us. Yet they were entrenched with our enemies as deep as any such battle before us. But we shall again go to the fires and bring along the drink and tobacco carried the long way from the sands and the shore to the south. We shall again ask their permission to remove them from this sacred place or to show us the way to make peace and live again as brothers. It will not happen this day, as it will be a busy one using hoe instead of hawk, so we all must be patient. We must dig them deep into the soil so no trace will remain for the coyote or bear. Yes, we toil today, and we will send these people on another journey, but I much prefer to send their braves on these travels instead of my brethren. The sun cannot set on their faces this day, as they must be well on their way to meeting the Creator before their spirits, now hidden well within them, are forever fetched from their earthly forms by our enemies.

Too many of our villagers will rest forever on their lodgepoles this night. We, too, have the trophies to show our fearless yet meager toll, at best by any standard. Before this is all forgotten, it will be heavy with them, and the scurrying dogs of the camp will come to sit and watch as the hair runs thick with our tribe's blood and be there as it eventually touches the ground, making it all run with the red no longer running in their veins. Their prizes and ours are the same. We give a quick death to their fearless and a low, slow torture to those who chose to whine or cower as we approached, for they are the lowly and must be separated from the brave or both will return to us for eternity as the creatures we do not respect.

Today we were not defeated as they believe. We were outnumbered and had to retreat to come to conquer them another time. The Great Spirit did not forsake us. He just allowed us to be human for the moment, and we shall be stronger for it. Although our numbers have been diminished, we will be stronger the next time and fight as fiercely as they have ever encountered. It is the way of our people.

Tekakwitha was still on the shore as the canoes returned. She was walking, near sightless, reaching out to touch some of the returned. I, for one, stepped aside from her approach, as I was not prepared to listen to her prayer of her mother, the "Hail Mary." It is all she can remember of her, but it rings constantly as she moves along the rows of longhouses, guiding her every movement. Her mother was the elder of her clan's women, and she is the princess who, with only four years on this earth, had suffered the pain of disease and the humiliation of the young men of her village. They constantly taunt her, but she never relinquishes her strong feelings for the Jesuits' lord, or his mother Mary, and she is becoming nearly immune to their rants as she grows older and a good deal wiser.

Tekakwitha has gained some in stature since her parents perished, now a few years ago, in the old village. She is still bent and scarred from the pox, yet she never misses an opportunity to reach out and comfort an ill child or a young squaw who has learned of her man's death in battle. She moves among us freely, and as well as those with the eyes of an eagle, yet hers are like the mole or porcupine that wander aimlessly down their beaten paths to destinations only they can know for certain, yet never in a great hurry. She speaks to the children and draws them away from the moans and smells of the still-dying men. It is she who shows the way to inner peace as some lie there with their chests laid open by ball or axe and watch their beating hearts grow silent as their life's blood runs thick upon these grounds.

Tomorrow we will add still more of them to the mounds and sing their praises to help them continue their journeys. It is now I must take time to heal my wounds and ask her for nourishment in order to allow me to again bring our clan together and again ask the spirits to guide us tomorrow. They have done this over and over again since the beginning of time. She is silent but always in sight. I wonder what she sees through those veiled eyes of hers. Does she communicate with the spirit world on her own, or does she believe what the Jesuits had taught her mother to be so? I, for one, do not want them in my longhouses, but it is she who refuses my wishes and brings them in and feeds their bodies. And they fill her mind with their beliefs before they again move on to the next village and then the next, until it is time for them to return, as many moons have passed along through the sky.

I, for one, find little use for their beads and prayers and cannot read their words. I, as chief, do not want their chants or songs spoken to my people. I, for one, do not understand why she alone can speak their tongue. I, for one, must lay my head upon the skins of bear and fox and close my eyes just for a moment. It, after all, is she who claims she sees them clearly in her dreams and hears their messages as those in the lodges sleep next to her. She alone always seems to be walking the fields with eyes upward and reciting the whites' prayers. She alone seems to have a glow of peace about her as she makes these journeys to the edge of the village.

I, for one, wish her a brave to snuggle with against the cold, yet she rebuffs all of them who venture toward her. I, for one, believe she needs to be alone at times, and I, for one, will not force her to change her ways. Yet I do not want her to spend any more time with these black robes, as I believe the sickness that took her parents and brother was hidden in the blankets and trinkets they brought into our camp as book and bead. But for now, I will watch over her and make sure no harm comes to her. I know she does not have any hatred in her heart, and the children all cherish her as she cherishes them. But for now, I must close my eyes to her. Perhaps I will see the visions she claims to see, and I will understand her ways all the better. Now I must rest, for we begin anew on the rise of the sun tomorrow. Now I must sleep. Her chants are constant and sound so sweet.

Oh, my brother's young daughter is now of my own lodge. I can never truly refuse her, yet I cannot accept her as she exists. She, like all the children, must learn the ways of the squaw, and she appears to be willing enough, but she ventures out to learn the ways of our young braves as well. She appears to accept her place in the near-sightless world around her, and little prevents her from growing old and helping with the chores. Of course, she still finds her mother's incantations and precious wampum beads to be a real value to her daily life here.

She finds a peace under the blanket she places over her head to prevent the rays of the sun to further injure her eyes. She is good at fetching the water, and she tends the small shoots and brings them into the fields when they are ready enough. The corn of her field is taller than she is, and yet she continues to haul pail after pail from the lower spring. The quenched earth appreciates her offerings, and the corn will grow thick and yellow as the summer lingers into the change of the season and the trees grow bright and fall slowly as the day draws to a close.

She alone takes up the beads, the same beads held sacred as her mother, Kahontake, prayed to Mary upon. Her mother is now lying dead, with her son pressed to her chest. They both took their last breaths from the same pox that scarred the little girl severely upon her face and neck. She no longer has the beauty of her childhood and no longer resembles her mother, yet there is still that radiance about her just the same. She can see through the clouds and stars above, all the way to her father's house. Yet she cannot see the trees clearly out in front of her, for she must walk with outstretched hands, feeling her way along an unfamiliar path. Her counting of the footsteps allows her to venture out around the village without so much as the slightest of hesitation. Her smiling face never sees the worry we have for her, yet I know she must sense it anyway. She is needed to tend the crops and fetch the water, but if she disobeys me, she will be laid down with her parents and the young one if she so much as brings shame into my lodge, and that is my word on this.

We are a smallish clan, but we are the Clan of the Turtle, brothers to the Wolfe Clan and those of the Bear. We are a proud and fearless tribe of the woodlands. We are a band of hunters who seek our prey and fish our streams below the great falls of the rivers that abound around us. Our women can grow great quantities of corn, squash, and beans enough, so we can be most generous when we bring it into the village, as all is shared with those to come to sit at the ring or toil in our routines. Those who sit and squander the day will go without, and to this, I am adamant. We do not reward those who are lazy or disrespectful. Those who disobey our kind can be stoned or put under the spear or club, and those who disgrace their men are quickly dispatched and never spoken of again. Nothing I say must be dishonored or I will lose my place as chief.

We do not wish to war, yet we must or perish here and now. We will not become Algonquin and lie with these whites, for we are Mohawks, and as one of the five bands of the Iroquois, we can only hold this ground for a short time before another great famine or flood drives us ever further from our ancestors. I will not surrender this place to another. We will seek the next bend of the river to make a new camp if we are forced to move on. But today I sit here on my haunches and rest, for when I look out of the lodge's small opening, I see her as my new daughter, Ioragode, and to me, she is the most beautiful thing of all I survey. I am the fortunate one, and I can learn a lot from her.

Father Lamberville in the wilderness

Prayer of the Prairie Flower

Oh, heavenly Father, I worship you this day,
I have walked alone without benefit of my earthly family
since their passing so long ago.
But I never walk alone through the fields of sage and grasses,
for I have taken your hand,
and you guide me in the light of the day or the thick of the
deep snow.

Oh, heavenly Father, I seek Mary as my guide,
For she knows me well and comes to me in the night sky
before the fire has grown cold.
She comforts me and shows me her face and extends her
hand to me
And soothes the pain in my heart.

Oh, heavenly Father, I worship you this day.
You have made a place for me beside you, and I will be there
soon,
For I need to see my mother's eyes and hear the cry of my
brother.
I worship you and all you hold true. I cast out all others.

Oh, heavenly Father, I walk blind and weak this day,
But the joy of seeing you will carry me away.
I seek the face of my father upon the fields of wheat,
But it is you, my heavenly Father, that I'm walking out to
meet.

Oh, heavenly Father, I hear the sounds of the owl.
Where he has been, I do not know.
But today he carries me home and the faces of all those who
left me behind.
I am once again sighted and can see the flowers in the prairie,
and each one has a familiar name.

Oh, heavenly Father, if my time comes today,
I wish nothing more than to hear you say, "Come home, my
child," and I will run through the fields of prairie flowers with
them all once again,
For I live only to serve you and Mary until my very end.

Chapter III
Strawberries, Summer Squash, and a Thing Called Smallpox

Oh, Mother, why is this so?

I, Ioragode, remember my parents and honor their memories every day of my existence. It now has been years since I touched their flesh, yet I can sense them within me. They are everywhere I roam, they appear everyplace in my daily thoughts, and surely they are in my prayers to Mary. I see glimpses of them as I stop along the paths. But they do not stop to talk with me.

I am Ioragode, firstborn of union of the great Mohawk Chief Kenneronkwa and his captured prize of the great native wars. It was he who claimed her now for his life's companion. She was Kahenta of the Algonquins to the east. She is said to have been a princess as well. To this, there can be little in the way of doubt. Her father and brothers were all surely killed in battle or they would have come to fetch her back long before her death. But now, sadly, both she and Father are now still. I can see them stretched before me without benefit of motion. She is so silent, yet a peaceful look is on her loving face. Her lips are still, and she remains without any breath or clearness of eye. Yet there is an aura coming from her. It appears she is just sleeping, but I know better. I lay next to her under the robes of the bear, touching her now-cold skin and rubbing her face with mine to catch even the slightest of life within her. It was not to be. She is lost to me.

Oh, my dear mother, Kahenta, your earthly body is here only to be seen by me. Must we lie together in the awful smoke-filled air of our longhouse without yet the aroma of the perfume that the fire of birch bark and the sweet balsam brings to you? The mat you lie upon has lost its needles and should be changed. No more is the smudge pot lit, yet its aroma still clings to all it has touched. Like the fire in the ring before us, your life has grown cold and no longer exists. Your hair, once as shiny as that of the bear's eye, no longer has any luster. Your pleasant smile allows the reflections of your soul to shine through. I feel your spirit is now and forever severed as if taken by the sharp blade of Father's hunting knife. I must withdraw from you, yet I will stare into your beauty one last time to allow me never to forget you. Oh, Mother, why is this so?

Oh, Father, the nation's leader of the Turtle Clan. You were the sole protector of this Algonquin princess who lies next to you. He was always loyal to mother ever since she was a mere girl like me. He could claim many as his prize, yet he chose only her. I know the story as it has been told to me about how he kept her safe from all harm. This story now has come to me in a vision as I kneel to prayer.

He also saved her from a destiny of slavery, death, or even worse—even the everlasting torture of those of the white camps as they raid and plunder and finally put our villages to the flames of the night sky time and again. Father said there was no shame to be captured but there was in the way a person accepted their fate. Mother knelt and waited for them to overcome her. She was beaten and dragged by the braves, and not once did she call out or cry for them to abate their torment. She held her head up high and walked with an air about her that caused even the fiercest of these warriors to back away from her. Father saw her qualities, and he alone came to the decision she was worth all of the scorn and trouble in his village until he could put a stop to it. He placed her among his aunts to learn from them. There she remained to see the Mohawk ways.

When the women of the tribe accepted her as a sister, only then did he return to claim her as his own. She, too, accepted him and went willingly to his lodge and remained there until this day. He kept her always by his side when he could and learned much from what she offered him in way of council. He was a big man yet humbled by this slight, childlike woman.

She was so small of frame yet truly a beautiful sight to all those who discovered her. As they approached, screaming and threatening her, she just knelt in prayer as they continued to advance swiftly through the trees toward her. She did not resist their taunts and was easily captured by the hands of the still-bloodied and fierce warriors. She was deep in prayer and had no fear for herself at all. She did not turn away but made contact with them.

55

She was sure they met her eye to eye so there would be no misunderstanding about her intentions. Many of her village were not so lucky. They bolted and were hunted down, almost to the last man. They were slaughtered, a few led back to the camp tied together like campsite dogs.

The time was said to be early at the start of the great Indian Wars, and Father was a young and anxious chief then. Now the time has passed long ago, and few remember when she came to them and lived among them. It as if she was always of this clan, but still not all the memories have been forgotten. A few have remained to give me hope she will be always known. We were the tribe of men who fear no other. We have been chosen to be always the victor, and to this end, we will not sway. This has been said many times by the elders around our fires, and I, for one, have no reason to think they are wrong.

Our people have joined our brothers and sisters to the west and fought alongside the others of Iroquois Nations as well. We must rid these forests and hills of the many tribes that have taken up with our enemies. Some have come here to take our fish of the swirling waters and the bountiful game of our forest, while others are here at the demand of the French to claim what is ours. If we do not take their lives, they will surely take ours. We have done battle with them at the meadow in the woods. It is covered in their blood, and we do not go there now but walk around it. It is said their spirits are not happy and will rise up and cause those who dare to venture in to be taken from us. It is so near what we call the place of the three rivers but the

French missionaries call "Trois-Rivières." I think they have named it well.

We are the Mohawks of the Iroquois Nation, and we are the fiercest family of the Turtle Clan. None of us, not warrior nor child, would run at the first cry of those of our enemies as they begin advancing on our village. We will not flee from this place while their brethren try sneaking closer and closer. Some have even tried passing over the river to our west and surrounding us, yet none have come away alive. We will engage them over and over again and chase them through the countryside. Hunting them down throughout the forest floor is not an easy thing, but we can track their paths well. We often move ahead of them and must wait for them to find the way. And then we will rest until they are upon us once more, and it is here that many of their strongest and fleet of foot will never leave the lands of our ancestors, for we will always be victorious. I alone pray to Mary to save them from their fate. I will not take up the axe or blade, but I will not bend to their will either.

This day, we again prevailed in our attempt to stay alive. Those who oppose us are never as lucky. We have done this many times before, but our losses are many still. Yes, we again repelled those many warriors who have come to defeat us so many times without success, but we are not as strong as we once were. The drum and flutes signal us over and over of these great battles. Their tones echo and thump throughout our valley's cool night air. As long as they are heard, we will live as long as the birds and the sky continue to be. We are, after all, Mohawks by birth, and we have always been in this valley from the beginning of our times.

My mother, as it was told to me, was among the few captured but not conquered women who remained alive when the Iroquois raided her village. My aunts have told this story to me ever since I came to live with them. They loved her as I do and have paid respect to her many times with their own silent prayers. It was a fierce battle that occurred here to drive those of her tribe back toward the great waters. When our men came from the woods and circled them, they ran away, leaving all who followed the war party behind.

Father spared her life, as it was his decision whether she should be killed or brought to serve our women as a slave to them. He took her to his homeland of the longhouses on the hill, and he spared her from all those who wanted her put to death for not being Iroquois. They were said to be joined in a union of each other's being. Mother knew from the beginning that he was there to protect her from future conquests, and he was a gentle soul when it came to his people. He made her feel safe, as no one of this tribe would go against his will. She had prayed for her salvation, and her god answered her prayers. The great chief, who was my father, would always protect her from the harm brought upon the villagers of those who were defeated by both native and white intruders alike.

The beauty of her and the gentle ways of this "Prairie Flower," as he called her, pleased him in so many ways. He was gentle and calm with her, almost childlike at times. She alone could quiet him, and he became almost as helpless as a new calf found in the spring meadow when she was near him. He no longer was the fierce and hated war chief who made others tremble in his presence when she was with him. He was a proud warrior, yes, yet he, too, was known as a fair and gentle man. He was devoted to her alone and did not take the many wives, as did others of his kind. He could have had all of the women he captured for his own, for it is our way. He felt he must be devoted to her, and she was his only wife, and he never changed his feelings until his last days as a mortal. No other woman could have possibly brought him the joy she did. He was a good man to her and treated her with respect and fairness in every way.

When she, as his mate, or any of us, as his children, were drawn near to him, he would direct his attention to us alone. He would bear a great smile upon his face, always making us feel we were the only thing in his life that was important. And to this day, I believe that is how he saw us as well. Even when he was in council around the great circle in great thoughts of war, he would stop the discussion to lift me or my dear brother to his knee and hold us tight. This, I remember about the man I call Father well. All those other great men and chiefs seated around him would stop and wait for him to begin again when he was ready. They, too, respected him for his ways, but not all treated their own women with this type of honor or kindness. Some are not good to their families, and Father shamed them when he knew of it. Many say it was his great wisdom that made him a good war chief. I, for one, believe it is his great kindness that marked his place, not his skills with his weapons as most think. He knew how to use the emotions of others for and against them, and he used them always to his clan's advantage.

My mother's smile and loving affection for him were to be seen by him and him alone. Rarely would she be drawn by her emotions, and she always tried to prevent him or any of the villagers from seeing her true face when it was a matter of the heart. She was always a private person of kindness and respectful emotions. She would not be one who pretended to need him at all and was as independent as a native woman could be in her dealings with others. She could, however, trade with the best of them and always seemed satisfied she had given as well as received fairness in all the dealings. She became familiar with all types of goods and knew the value others placed on good workmanship and honesty with each deliberation. The others around her soon learned from her ways, and all became a group to be reckoned with. Soon enough, the traders became aware of her and treated her with the respect of a great chief's wife and not just another squaw upon the trail. This was a good thing for all the women of our castle. No longer did my people toil for little in the way of the needs they traded for. She made them all feel as though they were finally respected, and they were.

Kahenta, wife of this great warrior and my mother, is no more. While he saved her, as I have said before, she would grow to respect and honor him. Then she gave him the honor of bearing his children, but she never denounced her belief in Christianity and kept the loyalty of those who had taught it to her. This was something that surely could drive even this king of the Iroquois from his own lodge to seek the shelter of the huts once used for fishing to gain any peace, but he knew he was in control of all our destinies, and he let her be for the most part on this. There were battles between them, yet they were always over before the next sun rose in the sky. She long ago was taught the beliefs of Mary by those Frenchmen we now call the "black robes" and their brethren who follow them throughout our nations.

Often, at times, I have seen her waist deep in sweetgrass, almost hiding from view of those who distrusted her ways. It was here she knelt to pray. She always carried her wampum beads of purple and white shells strung together with the fine sinew of the great elk. These, she wore around her neck and did not try to hide them from view. Her beliefs, as she remembered them, all were passed along to me, as I was her firstborn child, known to her as "Ioragode."

This will of course all change today, for my uncle has decided I am no longer a mere child. No, today I shall have my new name—the old one, I have outgrown. He has not given me any say in this, and his decision is final. Today, because of our custom, I'm to be known forever as "Tekakwitha"—one who walks with hands outstretched. This is what my uncle calls me. I do not mind it though, as I have outgrown this childhood name and the taunts that came with it. This is how I shall remember them and forgive them for their assaults on my person. They are all long gone now, but my heart is still heavy. I know, someday soon, I will walk with them and the Curator of all. I am warmed by the thought of this. I am now the only child of these great people who remains alive. It is said I look like her, but I do not know that for sure.

The sickness has marked me, as it has my swollen skin so that when I look to the spring, even I turn away ashamed. But it is my inner peace that I look for. Each day, I find the little child in me, and it makes me get through the toughest of days. I remember the words of my mother as she knelt in her solitude. The young men again think I am for their pleasure and must take their scorn. I turn from their assaults and walk away so they cannot touch me again.

I will stand and ignore those who dare to come and taunt me, for I am the princess, Tekakwitha, the daughter of the great union of Kahenta and Kenneronkwa, and they will live forever within me. I, Tekakwitha, believe in his miracle, and the power of prayer will once again unite us all before the end of the days.

Oh, Mary, my baby brother is now swaddled in the pure white skin of a spirit deer, silent, without crying. Perhaps he, too, sleeps forever? She has kept him clutched tightly to her breasts, and he, too, is cold and not stirring. The heart of Kahenta has grown silent and as cold as the pounding stone, not the once-strong beat that had kept him warm. I still see the black robes as they lift him from her chest for the last time. He is motionless, without the benefit of a tear or the shrill of his now-silent voice. Yet he, too, seems to be just sleeping a peaceful sleep. The beautiful Kahenta, my dear mother, her human flesh still oozes like the sap of the maple in time for the spring harvest. Those once-strong-and-deliberate hands now limply clutch her rosary strung of wampum shell and tied with the rawhide of the precious elk.

She is near silent, yet she whispers to me a prayer I do not know. I hear her, yet it is as if the voice so powerful is one with the wind now. It is a call to prayer I have heard so often from her. She asks me to pray to the Virgin Mary as she taught me, the same prayers she once had been taught by those of the black robes before I existed. The words from her near-silent lips seem to be carried on the wind, but all is so familiar to me now, for I have been taught by her alone that at the hand of the white God, and his precious Mary, they would protect our people, our rightful lands, our deep and clear waters, our birds on the cool winds and those who flock to our fields, the tiny newborn deer suckling under its mother, and all the breath of our ancestors that carries away the smoke from the ceremonial rings. As we watch it climb to the heights of the clouds above, it brings us the purity of the snows. Then, finally, it is of the sleep time of winter, when all must grow quiet under a blanket of pure whiteness.

My eyes are closed this night, but upon the near-silent wings of kokokhas, our great owl bird, it is he that brings a chill to my inner being. And I rise to see his flight go right over my lodge. When I open my eyes, I see my father is well again and standing in front of me. But his image is that of his youth and not the man I remember him to be. And he is almost a stranger to me, but as he moves in closer, I know him well, and best of all, he seems to know me, and a smile shows across his well-tanned, broad face. It is a good thing to look at. I rise to face him, and I am not afraid, but he does not acknowledge me at all except for this smiling gaze. We stare at each other until there is a spoken word, and he again smiles and touches me upon my head as he did so many times before. I can feel the pressure of his muscled hand upon me and the familiarity of it all. From this moment on, he will again protect me from all that is evil and keep me as safe as if he were standing here with lance and axe. It is his way. He stares at me, but again he does not speak to me at all. I'm not sure he recognizes that I am his daughter, or does he think I am Mother? But I will utter the first words until he is made to understand. I am sure he will know me then, and we will be able to talk of when he, too, was in a village with his family. Oh, there is so much I wish to ask him. But he must bring on the discussion, for I know not why he is here.

"I ask ye, Father, the beloved of Kahenta, chief of all he can see and beyond. You are such a great warrior of the Mohawk Tribes that no one has ever been compared to you in all these years. You have not been seen by my eyes for many moons before now. Surely you are here to protect me and your little son from all who may attempt us harm or seek to claim us. I know you are a great warrior and you will do your best. But I must know about my mother—has she been with you all this time? It is I, Tekakwitha, who seeks to ask you to respond to me. I so long for your words and the smile that tells me all is all right with us again."

It is only after I have spoken that he seems to understand me, and then he looks at me and smiles and motions for me to follow him. Again, I ask for him to speak my name, but this cannot be because I believe he fiercely refused the words of the black robes and closed his eyes tightly to all that we can see with the Christian beliefs. This does not include him, yet he has come to visit me again.

It is my mother, Kahenta, who is now my spiritual guide, and we walk alone, hand in hand, along with my young brother trailing closely behind. He is no longer laced in the cradleboard but allowed to run freely of all that had once bound him. What a wonderful sight to see him running absent of his bondage, smiling and carrying on as we move swiftly along the edges of the meadows.

But just as quickly as they came to me, they are no more. All melt away as we enter the forested lands, and I see them no more. As I turn to wait for them, they have gone, and I cannot feel them close. I am alone again, and it is the feeling that the cold ice wind has come and stolen my breath away. My heart is heavy again as I walk back toward my lodge, yet I take comfort that I have not been forgotten by them. And oh, so soon we will all be together. I will remember to mark this spot with the cross on the trees, and I will always remember this moment as a special time. I am no longer sad of their passing because I have seen their fate, and it will be my chore to make myself prepared when I, too, am called to his house. But today I am to kneel and pray, for this has all been told to me by my mother long ago.

Tomorrow will be soon enough for me to return to the stalks that have grown tall and thick. I will carry double the water to them in the morning light to make them fat with the food of our life. I keep all this night to myself, for they of my village will not understand how this can be real to me. My dear uncle is short of temper with me these days, and he is not one who will stand for someone to disobey him. He wishes me well but will not listen to me when I ask him about my father. I do not understand his meaning by these actions toward me. Is it painful for him, too, that he is gone? Or is it that he cannot be reminded of his brother every day by the villagers and compared to his actions, both good and bad? Or is it that he wishes to just forget the past and rule in his own fashion? I do not know the answer to this.

It has now been some time since I last saw my mother and her infant son. I know this is true, as the trees have shed their color over and over again, only to be reborn in the spring of the year, with a new and vibrant green that signals all of the earth to come to life again My memories are vivid, though, and as clear as just a day or so ago. But my father, my chief, continues to come and stand over me in the deepest parts of my nights from time to time, but I am not afraid. I have seen him often. He just stands as if he watches over me, so silent but so real to me it cannot be a dream. I am not afraid of this but comforted in a way that he has yet to disappear as our ancestors have. He is still a force among us.

I remember seeing our elders grow old and fall to the earth. I remember those who caught the sickness and coughed until they bled. I remember the silent children carried from their still-warm mats and placed in the mounds to be taken by our ancestors to meet the Creator, with them as their guide. They are still so real to me. I could see the sweat upon their brows as they appeared in front of me, and

I continue to watch for them from time to time, patiently, for when they may return.

I am the fortunate one, for I am with them in their place and they are with me in mine. He who is my father comes to me often, and he watches over me in my days of darkness. I no longer miss him, and I am not afraid, for I am his daughter, and I welcome him to our new village, a place that was hard to find. He was the bravest of all of us, but he died in my place. Was this not his bravest act of all? Could this not, in itself, gain him eternal salvation of our missionaries, or will he just be another spirit rising on the smoke of the fire circles as we once again ask the guidance of the elders. He appears again before we begin a new harvest, and I am ready to take the journey to the great waters or strengthen the bows of the longhouse. Is it up to me now to keep out the winter and the ice it will bring? He, after all, is clearly here, but I know not why he will not talk to me.

The change of many seasons has come quickly again to us of the Mohawk. I remember little more than the foggy visions of those of the black robes. I had seen many of these men in my youth, making the sign of the cross with the two fingers pressed tightly together. Now here they stand again, high over my own body and praying to Mary, the Mother of God. I, too, hear again the screeching of the nocturnal and ghostly, almost-silent bird. Is he also searching for the great chief of the Nation of the Iroquois and the ruler of the Turtle Clan? Is he, too, seeking my father? I clearly can see that great horned owl now, with its arrow-like beak and long, deadly talons curled and clasping tightly to the branches of the pine, ever watching me as he surveys over his own realm. It is he with those haunting and mysterious yellow eyes glowing like the smoldering embers of fire that brings the message of death. Yet he is staring right at me as he rotates his head in search of even bigger or stronger prey. I do not fear him, for I am never alone. It will be his choice to stay or leave, and as the day draws to its end, he silently moves on his way again, leaving those who see him to wonder about his mission. His screech has been silenced before it reaches my ears, and as I close my eyes, he passes overhead, and thankfully I am not to be taken this day.

I again hope to hear baby brother's sweet giggle of delight as I swing him higher and higher in his basswood hammock. I had woven this bed with my own tiny fingers during the many hours of my mother's labor—she alone tutored me in her ways, and the fineness of it was something to behold. Oh, will they come again to visit with me this day? It has been such a long wait. I have been on knee since the rise of the sun, and it is now growing colder and dark. This day is at another end. I must not rest, for I have much to do before I close my eyes and begin this all again on tomorrow's sounds of the meadow birds and the caw of the crow as it is pushed away from its stealing ways.

It is when I took endless walks through the high fields and the softwood trees growing spindly below this place that I remember her the most, for this is familiar ground to me. I followed her as a child not yet old enough to accomplish much. We so rambled through the high sweetgrass and down to the soft ground just above the waters. I loved to watch the grass as it was bending on the wind, with her hair flowing behind her as she waded through it over and over again. To me, it was almost like we were dancing in gentle winds and she could wish it to move back and forth without any words from her lips. To me, this all was making it come alive around us in a joyous and delightful way. Oh, I miss her and will search for her face in my dreams forever. I know she is happy with her son and husband, yet she must miss me as I miss her, doesn't she?

As I lie here awake, it has yet been another sleepless night. The black robes come again to me out of my fog. I clearly see the three of them standing in our longhouse, but they have changed in some way. They are talking amongst themselves but still not looking at me. I don't think they know I'm here, or maybe they just don't care. I have a feeling I have never seen them before, but some things are familiar to me. They appear as the same three brothers of the cloth from my youth, but yet they are changed by the many seasons since they last appeared.

As I watch them, it is as if they have never left here or that a day hasn't passed since we last spoke of the Lord, yet this cannot be. This day and time, they don't seem to see us at all, nor hear the voices around me the same way I do. They are here to bring me even more spring water from the coolness of the pool, and it is dripping slowly from their hands onto my parched lips, down to my swollen tongue. It rolls down my cheek and into the blanket that has been placed under my head. I can feel it close as it runs wet with my hot sweat and now cools me wherever it finally touches the flesh. I am now moved violently again as I shiver from

69

the moment the cool, clear water again gently hits me as it is being poured so generously over and over my fevered brow. The sensation turns to a welcome one, and I appreciate the flow of the pure water as it continues to cascade around my face. My pain is comforted by what I have witnessed, and I sleep for I know not how long. Surely this is not the "evil medicine of the black robes" as Father once proclaimed. It must be something special to them, for they carry it with them at all times. I open my eyes to see that they are no longer with us, and I feel that I'm alone, yet my heart is filled with joy.

My Mary stands in front of me now, all adorned in her blue gown. She is so pure in the bright light she has brought with her into this place. I look into her face, and she is as beautiful as anyone I have ever seen before. I try to get up, but my body feels heavy to me. It is as if a great stone has been placed upon my chest to hold me to the bows below me. As I continue to struggle, I cannot move forward. Any movement is senseless. Then, as if I have been reborn, I am calm, and I can hear her words even though she speaks not from her voice. She floats above the ground as if suspended, yet she is free. I love her and want to go with her, but she says it is not time, but soon, she states. I will be with the Lord and all those I have ever loved soon enough, she tells me in her way. I will be in a better place than the one I am now bound to, that is for sure. And with a smile, she, too, is gone, but the light from her still lingers as if the sun has come to my lodge. Then it, too, fades from my sight, leaving me with a warmth I have never before felt.

The weight is suddenly lifted from me, and as I look into the dimly lit fire, I know all has come and gone quickly this night. All is right with me again. I touch my face and the scars of the pox I cannot feel. The scales upon my eyes have been lifted, and I again can see my way clearly, even in this darkness left behind by those who have visited me. With a great breath, I'm up and out into the night air, searching for any remaining signs of her, yet I am so alone. The stars in the heavens are dancing on the night winds, and each has a sparkle all its own, each bigger and brighter than any I have witnessed. There is a feeling about of wellness within me, and I return to my bed only to pray until I see the sun again climbing through the silver trees around my lodge. And as I begin this day anew, all that lies before is as if I have seen it never before, and perhaps I haven't.

As I draw the water for the daily meal, I see that I am myself after all. I have not changed at all. She came to me in the night, and that, I know. I will kneel at the crosses today and pray she comes to me again. I only ask for my mother, but I do not see her. I will try all this again tomorrow, and then again on the fall of the next day's sun, and then the next, until I see them all before me. We can run through the meadows together without the pain and agony brought to us on the blankets.

The long death of my parents and the lost sign of my brother have been brought to me night after night. I miss them so, yet she tells me they are safe and in need of nothing, for they are with the Christian Creator, and he is all good. Yet I cannot think of a time when I close my veiled eyes that I don't see them in front of me. They appear so young and fresh to me as I grow older still. They are not a memory to me. They are a new friend or a child who has cried its first breath. I will always honor them, and as I believe, one day, we truly will be together, with even Father there to greet me. He, too, will come and seek redemption from all his earthly ills, and he will be brought to see the Lord as his Father, as I do.

I will go into the woods again this day and make the sign among the yellow birch, for I will mark the sign on every tree until they come to me in my sleep again. I will fashion the crosses from the fallen branches and tie them with the sinew I have chewed for this occasion. My life is full of the fields of corn, the animals that scurry across my path, and best of the children who play a game with me as I walk to my lodge. But there is a pang of hunger growing within me, and it is not from lack of maize. I need to feed my spirit being until it cannot hold any more. Only then will I know of the ways of Mary and find my way to her through the ever-shifting stalks of the fields, the wondrous corn rustling in the gentle winds as the day begins again.

Chapter IV
The Cornfield

My child, I think of you.

She is there on her hands and knees at planting time, pulling the weeds and separating the stalks that have begun to grow too close. She is there every day of it and will be there again tomorrow, bent at the waist or stooping over as she reaches into the freshly made and so-well-woven basket of the sweetgrass. The scent of it still clings to its very fiber. She reaches into it and then retracts, bringing forth yet again another precious plant she has begun on the shelf of the lodge. Or perhaps today it is the seeds of so many ancient stalks that will be placed in a shallow furrow and tenderly watered. The vessel she carries was made from the best reeds of the logan's backwater, located not far away from this very place but still a walk made difficult through her veiled eyes.

Never does she complain or cry out in pain of her torment. She always appears pleasant enough as she carries a childish smile on her lips and a soft, kind word to one in passing. She has this basket filled with the seeds for a new generation of the maize of life. It remains well protected from the creatures who would consume it if it was in a pouch or any other place. It was fashioned by her own smallish hands just days before, without the need of any assistance by another. She has made time for it between her chants and silent prayers. This young maiden who has the deep marks and thick redness about her person not yet fading has clearly been one who narrowly escaped the death of the trader's blanket, yet she still does not tire in her work. Although her body is so frail and unassuming to me, she has the strength of many. She has taken the place of more than one of the young men who now are absent by war and death. It is she who does this willingly, without complaint. Their chores are fulfilled as if she were many, but this tiny girl stands all alone in her cornfield.

Others of the Turtle Clan have taken to their longhouses to rest from this now-sweltering heat of this day, but Kateri is there whether we oblige her or not. The time of the planting, like the heat of the earth, has come early to the river of her ancestral home, but still she works with a sharpened probe and hears the taunts of the young braves endlessly harassing her. They know little of her torments and only see the ugliness of her often-cloaked face. Surely they cannot know of her true beauty. She, for one, does not appear to hear their boyish howls or even be aware of their charging motions. Even the flung stones seem to miss their mark over and over again, and only occasionally does one strike her. Yet she does not retreat or flinch with its assault upon her. The young aggressor usually leaves her to her chores after he cannot move her to the tears he had hoped to see from her. She holds little in the way of fear and no hatred toward him. She does show one of her greatest gifts, that of tolerance and compassion, which can be read on her face if anyone should care to look directly at her.

After all, she is the daughter of a great war chief, and her mother was the most beautiful of flowers herself. Unfortunately, both are now long dead and forgotten by most. Some of the shamans say they have witnessed her walking with them beside her as if they have come to protect her even to this very day. She does have conversations with them as she walks the trails, and no one has challenged her about this. She is perhaps possessed or even thought of as being touched. They believe like many of her villagers that they must keep their children of the board from her view or they, too, will be cursed.

Yet the young flock to her side and sit beside the trail for her to reappear from her daily treks to the slow-sloping hills now covered in waist-high corn. They follow her along her path just to listen to her soothing speech, for they see her real beauty. They dart in and quickly retreat. Then they reach out to touch her worn flesh, running ahead with nothing but joy on their little round faces. It is as if they have a great game going on amongst themselves, and it amuses them so. With one call from an observant elder, they melt away from her and hide until they reach the village again and find their own longhouse.

She does not bend to desires of the men like her adopted sisters have, nor will she relent in her quest to save herself for her life's mission. They still come to suit her, yet she has little to no interest in their playful actions. She can be oddly beautiful in this early light as she sees her reflection in the pool at her feet. She will not make as much as a ripple while she wades the stream to reach her special place among the greatest of our trees. Again, it begins each and every day as the task at hand that once was meant for many is done at each and every sunset by the hands of her alone. She appears to be content enough in her way. She continues to nurture her fields day in and day out, as they always seem to blossom under her tutelage, even while her sisters' fields tend to dry and fail. She toils in carrying her bladders of precious water from the brook she has made clean and clear by removing everything that has been discarded and left to remain in it. Now its waters are sweet and pure.

The haunting sound of the young braves playing their first flutes rises softly on the afternoon winds. Its melody jumps and falls much like the animated crow cawing above it all. It is almost as if he, in all his blackness, is the overseer of this place and the harbinger of what will come. Perhaps he is attracted by the notes climbing to his heights as well. Or maybe he has been here before and knows the way oh so well. His view isn't different than that of Kateri's parents, she believes, and it brings a quick smile to her. Her eyes now close, shielding them from the brightness of the sun, yet she seems so at peace as she softly mouths the words her mother last spoke in life to her. It appears the warmth soothes her, and her skin almost looks radiant, yet her marks are deep and cloaking.

All the while, she presses and runs first one finger and then another over the beads of the wampum now cleverly restrung with gut and tightly wrapped around her palms, with the deep-purple hue of the shell clearly visible on each of the well-worn pieces. It is all now rubbed smooth by the hand of herself and her mother before her. The trickle of blood comes to her palm as she asks for Mary to bring her home, with her ever pressing the sharp edges into her flesh without thought of pain.

The traders once extracted a hefty price for these trinkets, but now there is little market for them. The chief has made them scarce by his threats upon those who use them to mimic the whites of the French village so far away. Even on that long-ago day when her village was alive and clearly the center of her universe, these beads would still be hidden from the sight of anyone who was not a believer. But at one time in her past, many a pelt of the beaver was given in a one-sided trade for them. Maybe even a count of five or more was not unheard of, and the trappers knew well to take advantage of the natives, for they knew that an elder, a chief, or even a young maiden could alert the braves of their deceit and kill them before they could reach their canoes. I wonder what he would extract for them today. They may well pile high to the sky above before it is said that they are truly enough to make the trade. But to her, they are priceless and the cost easy to justify if she indeed had any way to pay for them.

She is radiant in the rays of the sun's first light to anyone who dares to venture near to her. But few of her villagers ever will care to see her or watch as this young child seems to float upon this earth, almost as if she already has joined the spirits of her ancestors. Her motions are one with the breeze and like the fluid of the stream in all its glory. Her soft and beautiful voice carries upon the mist of the fresh morning air and lingers till the last of the day falls in a giant fireball behind the trees of the distant yet familiar hills. This place is finally still but never sleeping. The songs of the dove, the cries of the coyote, and the shuffling of the bear outside the ring of fire circles goes on, quietly unnoticed, as she has finally fallen asleep at the last of the known day, at last, with her precious beads still held to her chest. It will be but a short session as it all begins anew in just moments again. She eagerly awaits her time to rise and unselfishly serve her true passion and blessed mother again and again.

Where are the men of this tribe, all dark and tall? Where are the suitors who come to the skins to love and woo her? Where are the boys who threw the stones? They all pass by quietly under the cover of the night, for they know her to be a chosen one, and they respect her silently. It is as if they are the washer women from the banks of the stream, as they are followers, not a true leader among them. Yet they are the unfortunate ones, for they who walk on tip-of-toe, so as not to leave the narrowest of print in the spring soils, will not go unnoticed by her, just unchallenged.

Her hair has grown to reach the soil behind her. Even in braid, it is thick and dark. Her eyes are a peculiar green, not unlike that of a new spring leaf, and it is said they can pierce the souls of all the Christian tribes. Yet she does not seem to notice or care about the motions around her. She is, after all, the princess of a people long since gone, and she alone has their blood coursing through her veins. Her family is well known and still respected. Some feel her father, the great chief, will come someday to lead them in a long-off battle. The elders talk of his exploits and his unfinished business.

Her mother is said to outshine the stars in the sky and was as sweet as the honey from the bees.

But as she is aware that they stare at her and often point her out to those who have not ever met her, Kateri does not offer up herself and is reserved to their glaring, as she has remained shy and childlike to this day. As she finally comes of age, fewer people will claim they have never been blessed by her. Her purpose seems to remind them that even though she is a sickly child, the honor of her village will never be bent or broken by them. Her aunts have taught her the deeds that she must do to feed herself. Her desire to pray leaves us no choice other than to take the meal we have set out in front of her all away from her. She will go hungry every time she refuses to work the fields or tote her water, for we do not follow her Christian ways, and she is ours to deal with. It is not intended that we are hers, as she seems to feel at times, nor do we intend to change all that has been told to us for centuries. She must obey us, or surely she will be left behind when we move to a hunting camp.

The signs of her tortures are clearing from her pale flesh. She has most well hidden below her dress made of the elk hide. Most are the new scars she has begun to dig into her flesh. She hides her torment well by the pitch of her chanting growing more vocal. At some point, her mattress of the soft pine needles and cedar bows has been replaced by the torn bark of the rough oak. She is one we must watch and break, for she seems bewitched at times. Our shaman or those of the council of elders are to deal with her disrespect, but at times, I fear her mind wanders as well. She is familiar to our ways, yet she yields only to those of the black robes as they enter our longhouses time and time again. They are the carriers of the pox—of that, I am sure. And we will need to decide whether she is necessary to us or if she should be cast out into the winds and snows coming oh so soon. Or should she be forced into a union where her man shall rule her insolent ways? He alone should decide if she will bear him a son or die at the thrust of his own axe. We will not interfere, as it has always been our way. They will decide on her fate someday soon, but she is needed here today, it appears, and we all partake of the same water and meal now ground soft and smooth under her stones.

She is at it today, and we can see her clearly. She is walking again with her ancestors, and I, for one, will not draw near. She does not raise a stick or stone but only smiles and extends her hand to us all as if she is welcoming us to her home. She has toiled day in and day out until it would break the backs of our strongest men, yet she reaches out not for a hand but to help those around her. Even those who bear witness against her and have watched her receive the unfair wrath of the braves have respect for her. Many of our youth who will one day compete to be a chief try to use her in many ways to prove their worth and judge her, yet wrongly. Many of the older men of the village have now seen the end of their days, and the younger ones are always looking to fill their space. They will use her to show their strength, and I fear for her safety.

Oh, she has ways about her that make me want to stray and follow her, not those beliefs I and the others have been taught by the elders. She is always with us, even at the end of day while we are in council. She does her chores but is always reciting the prayers that are forbidden to us all in between helping others do theirs as well. The older women of the tribe continue to accept her help, and some even admire her, but at times, they, too, will shun her, at least when it is in their favor to do so.

Kateri is so mysterious a child, and we all have seen her only one way, as a smiling youth who will not refuse the needs of anyone else. She stands such a frail child, but we know how strong she is in her faith that her way is the only one she can truly follow.

In this sleepy time, she doesn't make a sound. No movements are ever seen coming from her. She lies quietly as if she is waiting to be carried to the burial place, but her lips give her away. She recites the prayer of her mother almost as if it comes as a breath. Unlike those others of her aunt's longhouse, she can be still without a sound until she again is awake. She is the first to arise, long before the morning light tells the others it is time begin their day. Sleep doesn't always come so easily to her though. There are times when she sees nothing but endless times of being awake and wanting to do more for us.

We wonder if she is tormented by the life she has led or the one she wants to be living. It is not for me to say, but she seems to be searching for things that do not exist. In the early times, it was her mother who was there to comfort her and caress her until she was deep in sleep. Now she lies alone in the darkness, with the pale light of a dwindling flame to outline her body as she is remaining prostrate until the early hours. She has no one to call upon, nor would she do so. If she was not so content in her search, I believe she would have been cast out of our lives forever.

The morning will bring another day in the fields for her. Planting time is never easy. She is quiet now. She will again tote the heaviest of our water bladders. The endless travels to and from the spring seem to refresh her and only bring her to smile as she again passes us upon the trails, always willing and eager to take on others' loads as well. She is never without a basket or bag in her arms from morning till the darkness overtakes her.

As the maize begins to grow, the silk is as fine as her hair. In the short time since, she has sown the seeds the earth has warmed, and it's in full bloom with her deeds. There will be a bounty again to bring in the time of the season change.

But first there is much work to do, and she is busy at it. Yes, it is clear there will be plenty of corn and berries, and the round pumpkin and squash. But she intends to feed not only the people of the village with the fruit of her toil. She has been granted a good life, she believes, so she will also leave a patch of the yellow maize and the biggest of the orbs to help the woodland creatures she has made friends with. No images have been planted or rattles to scare them off. She has always provided for them and visits their dens or walks beside even the skittish of fawn without an alert or alarm. This gift to them has become an offering of sorts, and we of the village do not interfere.

She will bring her aunts and the women of the castle to harvest at the growing season's end. The children will come, as well as some of the braves. It is a celebration that all clamber to join in on. Nothing but the fullest of baskets will be brought to the village when all the work is done. Kateri enjoys this season as she harvests the seeds to dry in the sun and pack tightly away, bringing forth the small, hard bundles only after the rains have softened the earth and after the snows have waned again. It is a cycle we all enjoy seeing, as the freshness of her fields bring us life and a desire to continue on. But when the gods do not smile upon the rest of the planters, we look at her with distaste. What is this magic she has, and at what price shall we all pay? Is she truly blessed or cursed? I, for one, wish her nothing but the best, but there are others who have neither a kind work nor a quiet tongue as she passes, again on her way to the fields.

Oh, she does the work of many, yet she is so small and frail. She silently moves along, day in and day out. The others of this village are proud to show her success to others without the proper credit given. She has had many suitors yet refuses to talk of marriage to us. We must force him to attend the gathering that she herself has prepared. She comes only at our insistence and constant calls to come with us to share the bounty. She would rather go to bent knee and whisper her prayers in the privacy of her own lodge. Others are forbidden to pray, but the chief seems to know it is no use for him alone to condemn her, as his niece. He would be discredited if he now reprimanded her in front of his people.

Tomorrow she will rise and continue her work. Many hours of the day, she will be alone and left to her own devices. Her nights are so brief but filled with the things the daylight left undone. Sleep, when it comes, is deep, and dreams of what is to be are vivid in her head, finally.

Her long days are without complaint and as long and hard as they can be, but she will be at it again tomorrow and the next day, for she only knows to serve her fellows. Tonight, again, she is at the fire ring, bringing with her many bolts of wood to ease the toil of the others. There is no other purpose to her than to please everyone's pain and bring calm to all those of this warring crowd. Her small purse of nuts and berries is all she will eat and share with the creatures who will venture near. But she will work with her aunts to make the most of the game and vegetables for the masses who have begun to crowd around this place.

The fields are dry and parched this day, and she will carry the water to them from the moment she rises until she falls fast asleep without even a prayer. Yet tomorrow we all know that she will be hard at it again before we rise from the pine beds and soft furs. She will circle her crops again and again to count the numbers and say the beads over and over. The well-worn path makes it easy for her. She can tread upon it even in the night as the last of the water is poured with her loving hands on stalk after stalk. The pumpkins are big and swollen and take a lot of the liquid from her and show little in the way of evidence that she has been there. But she knows oh so well which ones have had her attention and those that have not been touched. This day, like all the rest, her work is done, yet she would stay and do it all again if she felt it needed to be. The weather this summer is as hot and dry as it has been in years. She knows of the needs of the plants, but this night, she says it's all enough and heads to her lodge again, bypassing the fire and the family of adopted people.

Chapter V
Off to the Hunting Grounds

I have been summoned by my uncle, the great Iroquois Iowerano, who wishes to speak with me. He has had me brought to a meeting within his council hut instead of our longhouse, and I know not why. I have come into his place to speak with him and his wife, Karitha. She always sits beside him, but he tells me to be silent. I am not to speak. He is the chief of this clan and the keeper of the eastern door. No one can confront him without his temper boiling to the point of him becoming violent and striking out. There is always a sense of fear when I am in his presence, but I will not bend or bow to him, for my father was once as he now is this day.

I have nothing to be sorry for, and there is nothing I will change to please him, for I, too, am a princess of the Mohawk Federation and know my place, and I, too, must stand my ground regardless of the consequences. I come of my own accord out of respect for the station if not the man. When I see him, I can only think of my true father, who has now long since passed. And it sometimes takes my breath away, for it saddens me so. Father should be here, not his younger brother. Father was the great chief, not his younger brother, and in the end, it will be Father who protects us, not his younger brother. But here he is, in all his splendor, like a child playing in the forest and acting only like the native chief, but he will never truly take his place.

He makes me come in front of him as if I am a servant child, but I insist on standing in all defiance. He tells me we will be leaving this place with the great fence of security at a time soon to come. We will be gone but a few days, he says, and then we will come back again. It's a journey we must attempt to make, for we are ready to starve, for all our stores hidden in the ground will not carry us beyond a few moons, or maybe even less. We will travel along the river and go long into the well-worn trails of those who came before us. We will venture out until we reach a special place, where we will catch and dry some winter fishes and bring down many deer and hopefully even an elk or two.

He has told me not to protest, as the skills I learn on this trek will carry with me when I have a mate and when he and his tribe move along this same valley. I tell him I do not want to go. I want to stay behind and help those who will remain. I will feed the children or the elders who are too frail. But he stands resolute that I will follow them, and then he rises from the furs and stands above me. His fist is shaking toward my place, and he seems angry with me for something I must have done. It isn't my intention to displease him, but I know not what it may be that has upset him, so he is showing the emotion of a woman, not the way I believe a chief would act. He says I will accompany him, and he will not allow me to insult him in this manner. He says I am his daughter now, and it is he who must be obeyed.

I will do as he wishes, for he has been good to me. I love his wife, Karitha, as well. She has guided me often and tells me of her sister, Anastasia, who is a Christian, as I want to be. I can only see her when we are in the longhouse together, for she comes only so often from a village far away. I have learned the way of Karitha's lodge now and that of her sister's family. She has taught me to skin and bone the elk and deer and filet out the fish. I have bent for hours in front of the stone, pounding out the corn to paste to make the bread upon the fire. I have rolled the grains and mashed the nuts. I've picked the red berries for hours on end and eaten as many of those of blue color as I have brought to the village at the end of the gathering time.

We have chased the wild hare and run it down. I have sat on my haunches and plucked the great birds—the turkey with its spur and beard, the duck with its maternal nesting close to our reeds, and the goose with its alarm as we come close. I have cooked almost everything and occasionally had to prepare game that wasn't very familiar to us to see if we could survive. The snake and the snails are the less pleasing to me, yet some of us will eat the bark of the willow and the pods from the marsh and say they are as good as anything we have eaten in days. It is all edible if you cook it long and hard. She has told me that some of the men say they could eat the rocks from the riverbed, but I hope that day never comes because we will all be near our death if that should come to pass. I take only one egg from a nest that has five and leave the rest for their mother to tend.

I will never forget the teachings of her family and try to follow their guide, for if it comes to the wilderness or me, I hope I have learned enough from them to survive and to pass it on to those who come after us. It is not our way to kill just to show our muscle or waste a single thing. The Frenchmen and those they call the English destroy much and then let it all spoil, and then they will go without. We use the meat for food, we use the skins and feathers for warmth, and then we suck the rich marrow of the entire woodland beast to give us the richness our palate desires—and then we render the fat to keep us from going without. We will chew the sap from the pines to clean our mouth, and we will cook the bones again in our spring waters and drink from its nectar. We will dry their innards and grind them for medicine. I walk in the forest and bring back the herbs of life and health with me. They just brush it by or burn the understory to grow their own grains.

I must follow the tribe, for it is my place, yet I willingly go to the sick and the feeble and ease their pain, and now they will have no one to take my place. I think of you, Mother, and my spirit guide Mary without any thought of myself. It is our way to be one with all that is given us by the Creator, and it is against our ancestors to spoil or leave a bounty behind. We leave nothing in the winter snow except our footprints, and those, we hope, are only temporary. So when we find something that enriches us, we will pause and give him thanks, but I have more than one I must say the words to. My mother is always with me even when we do not speak, and she has guided me well thus far.

Today we are in preparation to leave this place for at least a little while, it has been decided. I must begin to gather that which will be useful to all of us. I have bundled up all the spice and salt we have traded for. I cannot imagine heading out into the wilds around us with anything less. I have never been away from this place as far as we will go. I have only listened to those who journey and the black-robe stories of other nations and other peoples who are not the same as us. I have a desire to learn of them, but I fear it may not be in our interest to meet on a new trail in their place. I know not for sure of the direction we will take, but it appears we will head to the north. We may go onto a great plain where the great gatherings happened in the elders' time. It is a place where the five nations all have gone to hunt many times before, and it has never failed us. We are of the eastern door, and we have the right to travel to this place before the others will come. We are, after all, the Iroquois and of the Turtle Clan.

The snows have stayed a long time this past season, and our short growing time did not allow us to carry much into the dugout of sod to stay cool and not rot. We will need to begin this journey in a few days, at best, for we will not have enough meat or stores to carry us until the end of the planting time. The river below us has lost some of her cover, and a few of our strongest men have traveled with its mighty flow and say the alewives have come and so have a few great fish. It is time. We must be prepared to find them when they come out of the lakes and head for the great waters, we are told. It is a long journey for them all, yet they seem to make it almost every year.

I have only heard of these journeys before, and I have never seen the men leave this way, or at least I have not noticed them. It seems that I must have never been chosen to accompany anyone before. I was younger when it happened, and it was not my place to go, or so I'm told. But this time, it is different. We are now small in numbers, and all must do a part. My cousins and I will take to the shoes made by my father. I now know why they were returned to me by my uncle. I have already taken them down from where they hang, and the gut has been strengthened.

We will be leaving soon, as the sleds we will pull are being readied. The men and women of our village will drag them through the snow for days on end. It shall be my responsibility to escort them and try to keep pace. Out from my hiding place, I see the squash and its seeds, and I add it to my things I will bring with me. There are skins filled with the nuts from the trees we gathered earlier in the season. They are all dried out now, and many have lost their shells. Much of what remains of our venison and bear has been hung in the smoke and is as dry as it can be. Yet the fish has a piney taste and is good to take as well. It has a sweet taste and can be added to any pot. All of it seems plentiful, except there is little more buried in the earth to feed us much longer. If we prepared a feast, it would all surely be gone, and without this journey, we would have nothing to eat, save for the herbs now plentiful and hanging above the smoke in our huts. We will fish for them at the place of the swirls and where the waters come back among themselves, and then we will journey farther inland to cross to the great river.

The sleds will be ready in a day or so. They are being loaded under a heavy weight. They will get lighter as we approach this place, for we will carry all we can eat. But they must come back full or not pulled at all. The fields of my daily walks are as far as I've been in my life. This time, I will be as far as anyone has traveled, and I feel a little insecure in the ways of the forest, but I, too, will pray to Mary that our trek will be safe. She will guide us, I'm sure, and return us to this place. The time is near, and it's coming to pass, but my part is so undefined. I want to be a helper, but what do they need from me?

My aunt and uncle urge me again to accept the use of a light canoa and a young brave as my guide. I will not be ready for him or anyone to call me their own. I'm too young for all of this, and I will not be forced. I will not bring them a bowl of berries to share, for I have decided I'm too young for all of that, and young I want to stay. If I do not protest, I will be forced to decide on a mate, and one I do not wish to have. My uncle is furious with me, I'm told by the women of our lodge, but it isn't for him to decide. I'm not a piece of hide or a canoa to take in trade. They have paraded me to the dances and to special affairs. They have dressed me in my fairest of skin, yet this is not the time. Why is everyone trying to pass me along? Am I such a hated person that they do not wish me well? Or am I so hideous they feel I will grow as a maid? It is not for them to decide. I will speak of this with the missionary priest when he comes near, for I want to follow Mary and my mother, and I want to hear him tell me in the confession if my thoughts are pure or wicked. I will accept his words when he tells me whether I am right or wrong. But I must wait until we return, for we are all prepared to leave, and I know if he should come to this village, it will be a quick visit for him. Maybe as I grow old in the way of the white hair, I will change in my ways, but to accept their advances today, I shall not be tempted further.

I will sit in the bottom of the oldest of the canoas with the other children set to go. We will be floating with the river's flow to the place we must portage and tote all we have packed over the height of land. Then we will again. He has sent some ahead to prepare the ground for us, and it should not be difficult to smell the campfires as we approach. I am told we will get there before the set of the first day's sun, so we can dance and feed the many who will meet us there.

We sought out the old village, the one of my father's, but all I can see are a few huge oaks blackened to their crown. No place of my birth exists anymore except to the occasional brother crow. One says he saw the owl hidden in the branches, but he was a young child, so I do not know. There was a big log stuck on the bank, and the four turtles it held remind me of my family resting on a rare occasion after all the day's work is done. There we are as the canoa passes father, mother, baby, and me—my, how we all look so content. As we watch them, they, too, disappear. First the largest one leaps for the safety of the dark waters and then the next until the log is bare again. Do they do this as if it is a game to play, or is it that they, too, fear the Mohawks? There is no sign they even existed except for my memories, and as I look at the once-flourishing riverbank that was once full of the lily, I see nothing else that tells me this is anything more than a dream. Oh, how the time has moved slowly for me. I search the sky daily for the signs of my family. I want to hear their songs and hold the boy close. As we wind around the bend, the old village again disappears. Did it really exist as well?

Can I get the oarsman to make a little stop? If I could get him to just put in for a moment so we could stretch our legs, but when I ask him, he does not acknowledge my wishes. To him, it is a place to stay away from, and he holds fast to the paddle as his eyes seem to be searching ahead for signs in the river that may alter his course. We are now beyond the place where we could return, but if I keep asking, won't they want to come hear the tales of my father and his greatness from his very shore? I, for one, must remember the tales told of the fire rings and the smoke. I need to hear them often, and by others of our kind, so I will not forget. I need to see your faces, for they might fade away.

I, for one, would be happy if we just had stopped to bow our heads, but it was not to be. I feel this brave is annoyed with me. He is one who has held the stones but did not care to let them fly. I see him only when he returns from his trips. He never come close to me when I am on the paths. They say he has many pelts and would be a good husband for me. But I think he is one I bear to keep an eye upon, for if he will pick up the stones, wouldn't he want to see them soon take flight?

We have journeyed long into this day, and the coldness of the river still edged in her ice has made us all want to move away from its banks and stand again on the firm soil. Maybe the feeling will come back to my legs soon. I hope it is so. But we will sit here for a bit more. It will take us a little longer to reach the foreign shores. And then, when we finally get there, we will be needed to help make the camp ready for the night. We must be getting close. I can smell a whiff on the cook fires ahead, and it is thick in the air around us. It may be another's tribe, maybe those of the wolf, but I think we are all alone. There are talks around our camp that the English have moved our way, but I have yet to see one of them within the trees watching us. I wonder, are they different from us? Are they more like our missionary French, or are they truly like old women as the young braves have said?

We land without much of a ceremony, and by the time we reach the fires, all those who rode downstream with me seem to melt into the woods. Darkness cannot be far behind, and I will surely want to sleep, but right now, I kneel in prayer and will be busy for a while. If my aunt should call out to me, I will of course respond. It is our way. I want to obey her and will carry on what she will ask without any thought of myself. She may want more water or to scrounge up some logs, but we will not be at rest until we have made this day's camp all well and good. It will be our task to prepare for the following day, and then and only then will we go to the wigwams and sleep until we watch the sun rise again.

We will begin with fish and the remaining berries. I will cook them in the pots I have brought. Mother's shiny one isn't here. I wish I had asked for something more from them to remember her memory well. It could be something other than the book and the beads. I am not saying those who have received her things are not worthy, but I was just a child when she left, and today I stand here with the women of our village as one of them.

Oh, Mother, I have turned the pages of your small book until they are so thin that even in my poorish sight, I can almost see you through them. I have prayed to the Lord and Mary upon your beads oh so many times that they now crumble in my hands if I am not careful. The colors are fading from the shells, and until they have nothing to hide, I will use them again and again. The men are around the fire and content. They are smoking their pipes and sharing the pouch. All things native are in short supply. We will need to have a great harvest to make this famine go away. The warriors have turned in to their huts. Some are already calling for their mates. I, for one, will spend some time staring at the embers a little longer in hopes the memories of my youth will again glow clear to me.

Many of us will sleep under the stars. Some have set up their massive hides. I have chosen a lean-to that lets me look into the sky. The small fish they caught today will not feed this camp. Maybe tomorrow the run will be better and fewer will escape the traps. It is time to say my prayers and remember those of my youth. I honor them in my prayers until I happen to fall asleep.

Our women will take turns hauling the well-laden sleds following the broken trail of the hunters. The men will wear the shoes made by their own hands, and many will make sport and race each other down the loosely defined trail still covered in the deep snow. There are others about, but we have not seen them. I have spotted the tracks of the lynx and porcupine. The coyote is here, and I think it is the sign of our friend the beaver hauling his tail along the frozen earth. We must be near his home that he has cut from the trees. I have a good time watching them cutting and hauling and building their great dams. They never seem to tire. It is told upon the fire that the waters to our north were put there by these great beavers. It is said it was long ago, so he could float his giant trees. Our ancestors must have loved to watch this sight as much as I do.

I cannot be out in front. I am too small and cannot see to keep to the trail, but I can bring up the last and follow the widened trail. They have worn it to the top of the earth. I have carried the snowshoes of my father a long way now. I don't think I will need them today, but maybe tomorrow if we don't reach the hallowed grounds.

The crack of a few muskets pierces the cold air with a sharp and clear report. I think they have brought down the game they were seeking. The tracks of a few men split off from our trail just a while back. I wondered where they were headed, and did they see something that should not be there? I cannot follow them, as the distance between their shoes is truly a great one and I cannot run in this snow. I am hoping for some fresh game to roast on the cook fire. The smoked flesh is so dry it does not chew easily. I will wait here until they come from the forest. Is it a deer or a bear? I will wait until I recognize them, for I cannot interfere with the way of the natives. It is not my place. They will carry the kill to me to take care of, and I will be happy in this chore. It will not be long because we waste so little.

I hear their voices coming from a place near, it seems, yet I still cannot find them. All seem cheerful and loud. There is no need to remain silent once the musket has been fired. Their sounds carry throughout the valley as they approach me. I can make them out now, but none are that familiar to me. I know they must be of our village though. I am interrupted in my prayers, yet I do not mind, for I am willing enough to do them over again when I am alone. I have a chore to complete now. I will open the carcass and roast the liver. The back will be torn from the bone, and all will have a sweet taste. The heart has already been cut from the flesh, and those who brought the animal down all have partaken of its juices. Each of them has tasted it as it was still beating. They claim it's part of the rite of passage, yet I feel these mere boys are showing off. The liver will be dried and ground to a pulp. I will add to it from my pouch of sage and lilac. Each of the men will now fill his bowl and drink the liqueur from its veins that we mix with the milk of the last lamb.

These boys who accompany me want me to give in to their charms. Some have brought me gifts of pelt and stone. Others have traded for the Frenchmen's metal. Others still claim I promised them long ago, but I have not been with them now, nor will I ever. I am not happy with their peculiar ways. Some stand forceful. Others just walk away. I want to follow the monks and learn their prayers. I have heard their stories of women who marry God. I think I want to be one of them. Until I decide, I will not share my bed. This is for me to decide, not the chief or the women of my longhouse.

I wonder what is happening back at the castle this day. There are so few of us who remained to look after them all, and I hope they are being well cared for. I have told them the stories as they were taught to me, but I'm unsure they will recite them, in fear of being overheard by the ones who will go to the elders with their stories. The children will do their lessons in the woods. I have left them a few prize crosses just outside the walls to go to. And if that isn't for them to do, I have carved the cross in the longhouse doors as well.

I hope Father Lamberville has made his rounds, for if he is there, I'm sure all will be well. He will look to their health, and he will bring them all peace that starts with his prayers. But he will look after their flesh and heal old wounds. He brings us the news from our brothers to the north as well. I used to visit the Hurons' place with him to hear him say the Mass.

We have few slaves that they still hold as their captives now. Many have died, and some we let escape. I do not think we will be seeking more, from what has been said. They have all been blessed and hold service right in their hut. Even our chief, my uncle, does not interfere with this.

My mother's sister comes from another village not far to the west to sit with this missionary and speak of her sins. He is welcome in my house. I have been warned by my uncle that I must not go there without a Mohawk warrior with me, and I will not do this.

They are known to sing out while they work our fields without a worry of death. Why am I treated differently than they are? This, I do not know. Some have been tortured, and a few even put to death, but they refuse to denounce their faith. And all truly believe that what they have been taught is the right path to follow. It must be something to be willing to die for a belief of a person you cannot really see.

I must talk with the missionaries more than I do, for I believe they hold the reasons I seek but have not asked them for. Maybe I will be anointed as they tell me I should. The way of them does not come easily to us of the forest. They will take much time to teach us their ways, and in a place that is always changing and under duress. I want to honor Mary and will do that until my end of days. Until I return, I will not learn anything new about my place in eternity and the beautiful woman called Mary. I must get back to the village soon, as I have only a short time to be here and the end will come soon enough.

We will continue to the river we seek tomorrow, and then I do not know where we will follow. The men are enjoying this adventure, and we could be moving until the signs of the lilies come from the thawed ground. But I think we are near our quest finally because he has sent out runners to gauge the distance, and they have already returned from the paths of the early morning.

The women of my village think I am ugly and should hurry in taking a mate. I do not dress to catch a boy or dance with them at the great circles. I make the clothes as fine as I can, for my mother was my teacher, and so is my aunt. They wore the best our village has seen, but what of this finery do I need to tend the sick or go to knee in the fields? I do go to some places, but it always ends the same. I refuse their advances and walk to my house alone. It is just not time for me to decide this.

I want to know everything there is to know before I make that decision. I want to ask the birds in the sky some questions. I want to watch the tall corn grow. I want to see the fishes under the river and hear what they say to each other. Why does it snow only in the season of the winter? Why does a baby have to cry to catch its first breath, and why is there so much pain for the squaw when he finally comes from within her? Shouldn't that be a joyous time for both mother and child? I have so many questions and need to know it all. Why do we walk this earth before we go to the heaven? Why do I see the visions of my future in the night but no one will speak to me—they just smile and walk into a blue light?

I am the adopted daughter of this chief, and he has told them I must begin to prepare for the time when I will welcome a man into my place to lie beside me as he does with his wife. Does he forget that we all are under the same thatch? I will not relent in my quest for the Virgin Mary or the Lord. I will honor my uncle only to a point. Then I may follow the priests to their northernmost village and hear the words I seek spoken openly as the claim. Oh, I want to obey those who guide me, but they must come to me as welcome thoughts, for I cannot relent in my quest.

I will sleep in the open, next to the sleds. I have spent the day's end watching the children who came with the women. I teach them a hymn and a short prayer. Some have heard them before from me, and all are quick to sing aloud. I am at peace with my decisions, and as I pull the robe to cover me, I hear the sounds of the fire ring and the men who still sit and draw on their pipes. Surely they have little tobacco left and their drink has clouded their visions. All should take to a mat or skin if we are going to move on tomorrow. We must be ready, as the new day is about to begin. I will prepare more

meat and some squash for their meal. I will use up all we have
brought with us.

One brave has woken early, and he comes to my aid.
He totes the water from the stream in the woods. His
brothers begin to heckle him, and he responds vocally to
them as he drops the skins and walks away. I look at his eyes
and thank him for his kindness anyway. I will bring the water
from where he left it, for it is a task I do well.

As they wake, they shrug off the snow that fell
throughout the night. It is so cold yet crisp. It sparkles as if it
is the scales of the fish we seek. Today we will journey farther
still into the wilderness that has seen few of us. It is said that
we will reach this place we seek before the sun closes this day.
The place of our ancestral village is where we seek. They have
sent us signs, and we will follow the trail they lead us on as
soon as we can break from our camp. Again, he has sent the
scouts out in the early light. All volunteered to be the first to
find the place. My uncle has been there, and he smiles as he
sees them leave. I'm sure it isn't that far, for he seems in good
cheer. The long trek through the snow has been good for him
too.

For the women and their children, it has been a long
walk. The snow has been deep and swallows them up. Those
who leave the trail of the men are eager to return to it, for it
can support the weight.

I, for one, like my place coming from behind. I get to
see the animals that were set to flight returning. Even the
great bear peak from under the stone. They have woken from
the sleep and will be out in the sun of today, perhaps to catch
a hare or look to the river as well. They don't seem to be

afraid, and I, for one, will keep them ahead, for I will not survive if they sneak from behind. The raven up high is watching over us. He is in splendid voice and shows us the way. I'm sure he is an ancestor, but of whom I do not know. I will listen to the stories of the smoke and learn his name. The birds are chirping and leap from bud to bud. They are finding plenty to eat, and it is a good sign.

I walk by myself with the sled still in tow. Its weight is not heavy, for I do it of my own will. I have marked the trail with the sign of the cross. I have made so many I cannot count them all. Those who may follow us will have an easy task. If they keep to the sign, they will not pass us and be lost in the trees. I'm hoping to find some new people while we are here. Maybe they know the words of the monks and have been to the north. Can I see them, not at this point but as I come around the bend? Maybe they will be there waiting for me? My village is moving swiftly now, and I see their tracks, but if I go off this way, do I have a chance to find others who seek the same place?

The redness of my flesh has slowed me down. The snow is deep, and I must now take the time to sit and pray for a moment. I will rub the skin of my legs to see if I can bring them some warmth. It does not hurt, but I fear they will grow too cold. I do not want to be left behind in the great woods to die. I want to continue to help my people and learn their ways. I must get close to them before we end this trip. I think if I travel faster, I will find them soon! Oh, there they are! I was not far behind. Maybe I will wait here a moment and kneel in the snow, for I am thankful I was not lost, and I need to say the words that will make it all right. I will help them with the meal and work until I sleep. Once they begin the fishing, we will not be allowed to stop. I will need all of my strength to help with the chores out in front of us. But tonight, we will give thanks and dance around the flames. They have brought many drums and a flute to sound the wind. I love this moment and want to be close. We will serve the warriors first, for it is now up to them to bring home the catch we will smoke and dry and roll in the skin. I know we will take only what we need and leave the rest for others. They will be here soon, for I have marked them a trail, and if they find a cross, they will know there are others who show the way to this place. And I, for one, hope they are grateful and they, too, take only enough to get them to the corn.

In order for us to survive, they have sent others in groups of two. They have been dispatched to the east, to the west, to the north. The trails they follow are deep in the earth and should be productive, but the trail is old and may have had nothing moving on it for many days. All the tracks are heading in one direction as if they are herded up, and the hoofprints are now made of ice, so they will be easy to follow even when the wind and snow cover everything else.

One lone hunter is sent to where we came from, to see if the animals have returned to the quiet place after we passed. And he is our best one, for if he can come upon a deer or such that has already run away, it may be tired and wait for him to pass. He is young but spends his time in the wood. He has gone for days without the sleep we need when he is tracking a beast through the forest. I have never seen him return to the village without a great harvest hoisted upon his shoulders.

All that they bring back will be cut and smoked today. If they are gone too long, we will send others to go to them with their blades, for if they do not return before the set of the sun, they have gained on the pack and brought some down. We will all rejoice at the camp this night, for our hunters are returning, some dragging a heavy weight. I, for one, do not wish these animals their death, but if we are to survive, we must take some to feed our bodies. Father Lamberville told me his sermons and books are food for the soul. I will ask him to show me one when we return from this hunt. I looked in the carcasses and found none in there.

It is a happy time for us, even though it has turned late into the night sky. But as the work is finally done, we all sit around a great fire and sing and dance. The flute brings us back to our time, and the drum's beat makes the heart of the warrior beat heavily within him. I have gone to my lean-to alone again, so they will not challenge me with their eagerness to mate. A young moose has come across the river and tramped through our housing. He will be brought down by the men of our clan, as they have taken chase into the night. They will screech and yell the curdling sounds, and I will wait quietly for them to return. There will be no rest in our camp this night.

It is a fitting end to this season's hunt, I feel, and I hope I am invited another time. I like the snow, all clear and clean, and I think the walking makes me better than I was before. I can breathe so much easier. I have spread the word of the Lord to all who will listen and left my mark on every trail I moved over. I like this hunt, for I can see the way of us natives is a good one, and we work as well as we can in getting the fish in the nets and the animals hung by the fire. If I was in the city on the hill with the Christians like the Hurons, I would still see our ways as being the best. If only we had a belief of my mother and the Father Lamberville, I'm sure we would all be happy and never go without.

Chapter VI
Lessons Learned

Oh, Mother, why did you have to go?

Here I am over here, standing next to this beautiful little brook. Do you think you have ever seen anything as mystical as its clear waters? It carries the life of the earth within its tiny banks. Upon it, I watch for those things that can float without any help for us. It carries many to the great waters far from us, but it all begins here, just bubbling from the ground beneath us. I have seen the animals bring their food to wash it here before they eat, and I've seen the mother doe bring the tiny fawn down to its waters for a drink. I am still looking for the elusive herbs of the forest, growing along her sides, which we will use and share. They are often found on the forest floor around here, but today they are few, and I have decided I will take a break from it all and say a little prayer. But I will fill my bag full before I go, regardless of how long it may take. Only then will I head for my home to refill the jars of clay to the top with them, for all to use.

I have been reading the words as they were taught to me by the Christian women of our kind. Mother, your little book is always my guide, and I keep it close. Anastasia and Enita have come to teach me the words that were hidden in the pages. They have become so clear to me now that I know not how I missed them. My aunts have taught me well all of this book's true meaning, and I will teach the children if they will only let me. They, too, were taught by the priest of the black robes, and other men of his kind. They have spent a long time schooling me, so I need to read the words over and over again until I no longer feel I need the book to comfort me.

I will someday have her words with me at all times. I will recite them when we all meet that day in his heaven. We have met silently here by the brook and have sat right on this very stone over there. Sometimes we hide within the cave on the other side of this hill when it is raining, but I prefer to have only the sky above me. I have learned it well, and I can recite the prayers to Mary almost as well as they can. The order of the Jesuits have come and made an altar to him within the village. I have not been allowed into the hut that holds it, as they say I am not worthy yet. I hope that with the passing of time, I, too, will be allowed to lie prostrate before him and hear his words. I look to the time when I will see him as they do, yet I have not been given a time for this to happen. I have looked for Mary to come for a visit, yet she, too, must be gone, for there is yet to come an answer.

Oh, Mother, where are you when I call out to you? Have you, too, forsaken me? I need you now more than ever, I feel, as I do not have the strength it will take for me not to give in to all their wishes. In your absence, I have been tutored by all who will help me understand all I need to know. I have spent time listening to the elders about all of the savages of the Huron Tribe to see if they can teach me more. I'm not afraid of them. They wish me no harm, I feel. We have them work our fields and pull the heavy loads for us now, as they were captured in battle. In time, Iowerano will soon let them return to their villages, we have heard, but no provision has been made, for who will do their chores after they are gone? In an old day, they would have their hands chewed by the women and then, just as they could not hurt further, they would be lanced and buried on the mounds with their kind. Few ever screamed out, for they prayed to their last breath for his strength, and it was given to them.

Mother, what would Father have done? I feel he would dispatch them quickly and without much mercy on the fields of battle and let them stay to rot. He would take some back to the village to work in the place of the ones of our clan that they dispatched. He was a good man, yet he was a fierce leader. I, for one, do not wish these weaker Christians any further harm. I feed them well and bring them fresh water from the spring. For a few of the younger ones, I have made their clothes, and some are adorned in the beads of my mother. And some have cloth from the French camps as well. I do not care for it, as it looks like the hair of the yard dog as he scurries away from being kicked. I fashioned a cross upon their vests to make them remember to pray to their master. Some will come to stay when the day arrives for them to leave. They believe this is now their home and become part of our families. This is a good thing, for they are sure to grow a family and make us strong again.

The black robes bring their own salve and medicines with them in their tiny pouches to heal their wounds. Some of it, I can smell from across the castle even before I see the men walking to the fields in the morning light. I, for one, have no need of this and will stick to the herbs of our forest. While all our workers will be gone until the darkness covers them, the smell of these so-called cures will linger far into the day. I would not accept it from them, but I wasn't asked. I have tried their quill and ink to write on the tablets they bring with them. I have spelled out my name, and the priest has entered it in his own small book. He calls me "Kateri" and leaves the "Tek-a-k-with-a" to others, for he feels it is more Christian and says it is "Catherine" as well. I do not know what he means by all this! I began as "Sunshine," and now they ask me to change again. Will I have another before I leave this place? "Ioragode" it was when the Creator brought me to them, and now I must learn how to say it well. "Kateri," he says, is my adult name. It is a good name, I think. But I still care for the name Sunshine as well. It is a good name to have.

The trees are bending in the wind. They are really beginning to thrash back and forth now in no particular rhythm. I feel a storm is on the way, and I have so much to do before we are again in the cloak of the rains. As I look into the sky, the scene I see keeps changing, and it makes me feel unsteady. My sight isn't as good as others, and the light seems to burn into me. I must cover my head on these days because the sun will cause me to be in so much pain. But the clouds will cover the sun soon, and I will have my pain eased. When I'm out and traveling on my own, I feel my way around with my eyes shut tight. That way, I can even travel these grounds at night, and I will never get lost. My people laugh at me and call me the child with outstretched hands. But I am a human being and want the respect they, too, demand for themselves. I work as hard as I can every given day, but it does not come hard to me. It is the way I want to be.

My parents were a princess and a chief, and they, too, worked with the soil and brought in the harvest. When they passed, I had already learned a great deal from them and have always had the thrust to know more. I have been a good student, and maybe it is my time to teach others of his goodness. I talk to the children when I am out of my house, yet they seem afraid of me. I do not really think there is one that fears harm, yet they have been told that I must be touched—a crazy woman who talks to the trees? Or maybe I am a woman who will never marry and will become an old maid, someone who travels and cleans the huts of others?

I, for one, know my place. I am a Christian, and I have my faith. I will never relent to their ways, for it is not as it is written. The good Frenchman Father Lamberville has taught me some. He and the Jesuits who have set up the small chapel for the Hurons in our village say they admire my beliefs, and it is good. But they, too, don't feel I fit their calling, I fear. I have told them I wish to join the sisters who live on the hills over the great river many times before today, yet so far, I have been turned away at every request. Oh, Mother, why is this so?

My sight has failed me this day. Oh, it's well enough to see their images moving about, but the shapes do not tell me who is actually standing in front of me. They are close to the ground, but I'm not sure of where they come from or who they might be. I again see these shapes moving about in the shadows, but no faces, yet I can sense them growing closer, and I do not fear them at all. It is my hope, if they come to stone me or strike me down, that it is swift. Not that I want to go today, but if they insist I should, I will not ask them to reconsider. Closer still, they stalk. The feeling is, they are so close to me that if I reach out, I will feel them, but I do not, for it is not my wish to scare them. I can see them now. They are the children of the village, and they, both boy and girl, are watching me watching them.

"This is a peculiar site, isn't it?" I say. "What do you want from me?"

There is only silence in return. I pretend that I cannot see them as I leave the confines of the hut and treat them as they have treated me. They again shadow me as I begin to find the gauntleted opening in the fence. Within a moment or two, I am down to the river and moving swiftly toward the meadow, and as I burst into its tall grasses, I fall down as if to hide, and I can see them still on my trail. They all stop as if struck by a great hand and look for me, but to no avail. I am invisible to them, and they all turn and run back to the safety provided by the fence. They think I have disappeared. They are screaming, I think. I have scared them again.

Oh, what a joy the children are to me. They are still so innocent and so bright. Father was right when he said we must have as many children as we can around this place, for they are the future, and if the screams and giggles and cries of the youth should one day fade from our hearing, we shall fade away with their silence someday. I see them often, watching me, but they still keep a good distance. It is my wish that someday they will again move closer. I hope it is soon, for I miss their faces so. I have prepared a song that teaches them about the Lord. I have made it simple enough, and I think they will like it. If I can only get them to come here when I call to them, it will be easy for them to learn. I hope they learn it.

But today I must prepare to go to the fields and pull the weeds from beneath the corn. I turn the squash toward the sun, and it, too, is growing well. I must go to the spring and tote the waters that give it all life. Today I walk without sight of anyone, but I am never walking alone.

I love to go into the woods, for they seem to haunt me there like the young of the possum and the hare that scamper around me in the brush, but not fast enough to be hidden. I get glimpses of them from time to time. None seem to care that I know who they may be. I think they have come to talk to me this time, but they say nothing at all. I call to them in a soft voice, and they run from my view. I am smiling widely now, as it is my favorite time. I will kneel at the cross that is now so well worn into the tree and pray to you, Mother, and to Mary while I wait. I say the small prayer I have fashioned for them, for I must know it well. It is my hope they will hear it and come to learn more.

I drink of the water in the skin I carry under my arm. The water is cool, and I am refreshed from it. I hold out the skin, but they refuse to take it from me, and they will go without. I know not how to gain their trust. They are moving again, and I see them clearly now. They are so close. I will keep my cloak above my head so as not to frighten them with my scars, but I fear I have already done so. There are many of them today, and I will turn my head toward them. I will not stand. I will stay here, where I am close to Mother Earth, and only move when I must. The youngest ones have crept even closer. They are talking amongst themselves as if I were not here. Yet they come and touch my arm and run again into the woods, deeper and where I can no longer see them at all. Still, some laugh as they disappear. Others, the littlest of them, seem to be screaming in a high, shrill voice. It is a joyous sound. I say the prayer as clearly as I can:

> *Oh, Father above, I love you so.*
> *Oh, Mother Mary, I need you so.*
> *Oh, Mother of us, I miss you so.*
> *Oh, my brother, where did you go?*
> *I look for you to guide me so.*
> *Come one and all, and hold my hand.*
> *Make me welcome here and in your land.*

I say this many times, and yet they do not return. After a long silence, I hear someone on the trail, and as I turn in the direction from where it comes, it is a young brave. I believe he is the same one I saw at the fire last night, but I am still not sure. I don't think he is here to lay any harm on me. His hands are free of stones, and I notice no weapons about him, save for his skinning knife, still in its sheath. He does not reach for it, and I again feel safe. He comes in silently and moves very close to me as if he is stalking his prey, but he stops short of my place. I am not fearful of him at all at this time, and I sit still as if to watch him as he will pass me by, but he does not. He comes toward me but not to threaten.

"I am called Mariachi, and I am Seneca. I hear your words as I walk the trails to your village. I have come a long way and seek food and shelter. I have been to the great waters of the Abenaki, and I wish to pass in peace. I am not here to harm you. I will not be here long. I have been taught the prayers of the Frenchmen at Kahnawake, far to the north. I am your cousin, and I seek the same of my ancestors as you. They were all killed by the sickness, as were yours. Mine came to their end across the great river but in the same year. I sought out your chief last evening for council, but he told me to come back this day. He and I have spoken before, but he still will not allow me to stay in his village. I must camp elsewhere and come to him under the noon sun. Iowerano feels it is the blankets of the priests that brought it onto us. I, for one, do not believe a god so worthy would do such a deed. Please say the words again, for they are all so close. I can see them peering from the edges of the fields. They are hiding in the grasses but ever watching you. But they do not stir from their hiding places, as they watch us for a short while and then retreat again to the darkness of the great oaks, and we hear them no more."

This young brave, Mariachi, moves to kneel at my side, yet I do not resist, but I will not move to let him closer. He touches the scars upon the tree and pulls his knife from his belt and runs it over the mark. It is skinned so clean and looks new to me. He smiles and then bows his head. He repeats the words I had spoken to the children and says it all the same. When he is done, he again rises to his feet and lights out to the place of the children. He is watching them to see that no harm befalls them. He is doing it without cause, for he is a true believer, and then he all too soon vanishes from my sight. I call to him, but he has gone. He has left a few shells of the tribe of which he spoke, and they are the ones of the wampum. My beads are now complete.

He is the first of his kind to visit my chapel in the woods. I hope more will follow him, for I believe there is hope for us now, and he was just one messenger. It will take many. He has left before the light of the new day, for he, too, wants to be home when his mother gets there. He does not want her to come looking for him, and he does not want to miss her. I so wish he had stayed so we could talk again. Maybe I, too, will go to the north someday.

What of these children? How can I make them understand? I have been patient with them, but they still stay clear. I hope to teach them all that I know, and if it is enough, some will follow the ways of the Jesuits, for they must be right. I have seen them so devout that they lie facedown in the snow, without moving and without benefit of the mat. They pray at every moment, yet they come to heal our sick, teach us their ways, and go to the Hurons' side of the great river to calm their fears as well. Then they go on to villages like ours. Some are close, and some are far away, but all are Iroquois. I would like to travel with them and meet my cousins, but they say that I am not ready and that my place is here.

Oh, why am I so longing for his word, yet it seems that no one is listening to me. I will rise from my skins in the early light and begin this all over again. I will seek them out closer to the huts this day. I will bring them the food I have prepared for the occasion, and maybe I will sit in the circle of life and wait again for them to come closer. Maybe I will repeat the prayer I made for them and see if they are listening. I will not give in to the temptation to quit, for I feel they are our life and worthy of being saved as well. One by one, they seem to come to encircle me. I know their faces well. Some, I helped their mothers with the birth. Others, I see their mother in their eyes, and there are only a very few I do not know, but they still feel familiar to me. They are the children of this great clan, and I must teach them the way of the Lord or they will be lost. I look for my own salvation in their eyes, and I feel they must have some good in them as well or the Lord would not have them come to me. I have little sight left in them, but the smiles on their faces are so bright it doesn't matter. I can see the way to their hidden souls, and I will say my little prayer again this morn, for they have me as their company, and I will not waste it.

Oh, Mother, this is a joyous day!

The children no longer fear me to be near. I have gone to the spring, and I see my face within it. It has washed the tears from my clouded eyes, and I see them all so clearly now. Its coolness takes away the fever that caused us so much pain and washes away impure thoughts. I have no marks of the sickness when I pray to Mary. She has picked up the chore of guiding me where you have left off. I miss you so, but I know I, too, will see you again when my earthly body grows tired. I can see them. Their clothes are all clean and neat. They are here, waiting for their lesson. Their mothers have done the best they can do with the sewing of the stitches.

Oh, Mother, I can see your reflection in this little spring. You are right beside me. I am comforted by your presence and outstretch my hand to you to again walk with me. Are Father and Brother near as well? Oh, what a glorious day. The children will be around me soon, and I must prepare for them, but I have prepared for this day for most of my life. I will set out the wooden bowls with the sagamité that is sweet to the taste. I made it for them with my own hands this very morning. It is from the early corn, with a bit of squash and some herbs that I have planted.

Many of the sweet plants came to me from the tribes to the western door, and I have so many that have grown tall here and now within my own little house. Still others shy away from the sunlight and adorn the edges of our field, enjoying the coolness of the shade. They all bring the color of the sunset to the pot, and it is a beauty to behold when the sweet aroma lingers high in the air as if placed there by the gods themselves. The berries are plump, with black and red staining the flesh in hues so beautiful. The honey of the trees sits thick and at the ready now.

My bread cakes are full and still warm from the fires. I move them away from the embers and set the soft dough on a warm stone, still able to feel the fire's heat, where they will turn a golden color. Oh, it is a feast for them, and they will come to the circle to listen to the stories of the goodness of the Lord. I will not only feed the body, but the soul will be nourished as well. Oh, it will be a splendid time if we are not disturbed. I, for one, do not wish them any harm and feel it is a good day to teach them. I will again recite the little prayer for them to learn its simple words and help them understand.

The older children will stay away, yet they, too, come in closer as I speak, but they still refuse to join us. They will partake of the breads and honey but dart to their perches once again and remain just out of my sight. I know they are there, but it must be up to them to come in and learn these ways. It is not for me to make them change, for I cannot. But when Iowerano comes to the field and demands all of us to go away, he spills the bowls with a swath of his mighty hand and raises it toward me. But I do not bend to his will. I know they have scattered, and many have run to the lodges of their mothers, but I will sit here until they return even if it takes a night or two. I am not afraid of my uncle, for he, too, can be taught. He will just take more time.

In a few days, I hope to see them again. They are so wide-eyed and ready to take flight, but a few hopefully will come in close, and one young girl named Kewani comes to sit right beside me. She is unafraid of me and touches my face and tells me I am beautiful. I feel she is such a special child and is as fair as the meadow breezes. She knows the prayers and can speak them to me without a mistake. I have few to give my sermon to this day, but if there is only one near, I am happy. I hear her voice singing the words. She has heard them well. We will sit together until her mother comes through the opening and calls out for her precious Kewani. And I again will be by myself but never alone when they leave.

Kewani's mother and I met on the path early this morning, and she is well with me to care for her only child. She wishes she, too, could come and learn the ways of the Jesuits, but it will take her more time. She has the demons within her and has lost her faith in the Lord she was taught about by the black robes who visited her village. The young boy who was born to her died this spring as the waters of our river rose around him. We all went to the shore, but he was not returned. The child's father is a great provider, but he will not go with the men to fish again. I fear he blames himself for the death of his son, yet he understands it was not his absence that caused this tragedy. I see him often staring into the shallow pool, but he does not enter it again. He prefers now to hunt the deep woods alone. I have seen him with his head bowed as he leaves in the new light of a quiet day. He walks to the trees slowly but does not look back. I think his heart is heavy and his native spirit broken. The Mohawk will not see a man with a tear, but I know there is pain in this one's eye—it is the same you can see in mine. If only he would go to the bent knee and say the words that will teach him, they will be joined again. But it will not be so. His daughter and wife will stand with him, and all will be born again someday. Why is this so hard for them to understand?

Oh, Mother, your favorite time has come again!

The women will meet in a great festival to decide our plans while the men will go away for a hunt tomorrow, and that will be a good time for them. They will proudly school the young in their ways to them. We will again be free of them for a short time to teach those who remain behind our secret ways and guide them to learn of our ancestors. The three matriarchs of our village—Karitha, the wife of the chief, along with Anastasia and Enita—will lead us all. They have all been chosen by the council of women again, as they have been in the past, and we are all happy that they are the ones who must be our teachers. They have the most wisdom. They were the same shaman last time, for it is their right as the elder women who watch over us all, and this is good.

The fire is now at its peak. Soon, oh so soon, we will begin to dance around it and laugh together. Its timber has been piled high to light up the sky above us and to show the way for the sky people to once again find their way to our village. I'm sure it can be seen from Mary's home as well, but when I speak of this, I get no answer. Many will see the glow, yet no others will dare venture close, for they know the signs that we will be together.

Other villages will hold these same ceremonies, but this night belongs to us alone. We have spent the day cooking and preparing the meal that we will spread out for all to enjoy. It will be soon, I promise. The Jesuits brought us some dried fruits that we have saved for this event. I do not care for them, but some cherish their all-too-sweet taste. I will dress in my best that I have fashioned with my own hands. It will be a white dress with the beads of my mother upon it. I will need to find others to stitch in their place, for I have used them all, and not one more can be found here. No longer is the small basket containing them full, but I will keep it close to remember her by.

We will begin at sundown, and we will check the tents, houses, and lean-tos, for the magic of our own circle cannot have a man witness or all of it will be lost. Enita, being the elder of them, will say the words of our native tongue. She, too, is christened in the ways of the missionaries and teaches us her own special way. But this night is the ritual of the moon, an ancient rite taught by one generation of Mohawk women to another. This is a rite of passage for us as well, as those spirits that we will see coming to the fire's embers have not been here for a while.

I rake the coals, and great plumes of fireflies seem to rise and race skyward from within its center. I do it again, and I release even more of these mythical creatures right in front of my eyes. They spiral upward and head toward the heavens. It brings the women of this castle close to its glowing face. All are ready to begin a night of stories, songs, and ceremonies just for us keepers of the longhouse. No men must witness us, for they will not understand, save for a few boys still being held close. We will all be hearing the stories of the ancient time tonight, a time when there is no land. It is one of my favorite stories, but it makes me sad because Mother is still not here with me to hear it again.

Some will shy away from the prayers that will be spoken on this night's sky by Anastasia. And that is their right. I, for one, cannot wait for her to begin saying them, as she has spent a few days alone trying to say them the same way the good Father Lamberville has taught us. Her sweet voice will bring all of the songs and prayers the life that the good friar could not. She and I have whispered them quietly many times in the longhouse. But she has not spoken them aloud before this night. She is excited—I can see, from the expression on her face—and proud to be able to recite these prayers. We have learned well from the missionaries and those who come to trade with us, but tonight we will not have them here to help us should we forget them. Tonight, she has decided, it is time to say them aloud in front of us of the circle. I know she is going to say them without hesitation. Her face is beaming in the light of our fire, yet she sits calmly waiting for the right moment. She will not be the first to speak out.

The eyes of the village children are as big and dark as I have ever seen them, half excited and half terrified to be involved. They are allowed to sit amongst us for the first time this season. Even the young boys left behind by the warriors stand with their mothers close at hand, but tonight isn't about them at all—they will go almost unnoticed. The young are all around us, some clinging to the mats, some in their mothers' arms, and a few, like the older boys, stand together outside the warmth of the great fire, just beyond its good light. But we know they are there and watching silently. Their likenesses are very apparent to us. They are, in fact, miniatures of their fathers, down to the three feathers hanging limply over their ears. We can see them as they pretend not to be listening, yet they lean forward to catch every word.

The older women are all seated now, snuggling near the fire rocks to keep the chill of the night from entering their bones. We are surrounded again by the boys of the clan. Something has brought them in close, but I know not what at this moment. They are the same boys who just moments ago stood beyond the protection of the fire. Now they have come close as well, sitting almost among the women. They will be going to their first vision quest oh so soon, and some will meet another night's fire in the dances of their manhood. This night belongs to us, not them.

Each of us is chosen to lead our village for what we can bring to the betterment of the whole clan. None will stand alone and survive, so we must band together and share our lives even after we have gone to meet the Creator.

While the men of Kahnawake go out and provide for us with the necessities of life, the food, the herbs, and the seeds for us to plant, it is, after all, our place to run the villages, cook the food, plant the maize, and rear the children. It is our place to keep the slaves at their stations, and it is our place to say when we are ready to find the mate we will bear children to. Our workers will live or die upon our words to the warriors. If there is one who displeases just one of us, they will have him put to death. There is no reprieve for our powers, and the mounds have many a captured Indian below their grasses.

This night, things are different for us. We will not have the men about. They will be gone on a hunt and have taken most of the young males with them. We will have our own drink, and the youngest of the maidens will serve us all our fill, for we have made plenty. Our elders will receive the choicest of the meat and the fairest of the squash and beans. We will again wait for them before we receive our share, but I know it is well worth the wait. It is all about to begin and I, for one, am so excited to be here among my family. I am somehow accepted as one of them even if it is for this one day.

Then it all begins with Enita and her reciting of the story of the Sky Woman. As she rises from her place beside the elders, all lean forward so as not to miss her words. She carries herself as if this is all familiar to her. I, for one, know of her anguish. She looks at me as if she sees someone sitting behind me that I cannot feel. The children are oh so quiet. They are good students. We are proud of them.

She begins in a quiet voice. "In the beginning, before there were the Mohawks, the Earth did not exist. But there was only the sky world. There was a pregnant woman who was the wife of a strong brave. She had asked her husband to go out and fetch all the wonderful foods she was craving. One thing she wanted the most for him to bring to her was the bark from the roots of a special tree known as the Great Tree. He had to journey far to find it in the middle of the sky world. It was a long time before he found it, and many forgot he existed. It stood there all alone and was bigger than anything he had ever seen. He claimed it took most of a day to walk around its great trunk.

"He knew no one was to touch this Great Tree, yet he wanted to please her, and he moved in closer to it. Then he scraped away all the soil holding it straight to reach the part of it she craved the most. As he worked, the soil began to fall away. It fell, shaking all the known lands, and its dust blackened the sky and made night. Where it once stood was a great hole, where there was nothing—no sky, no sea, nothing but the great beyond itself. As the woman drew near, she leaned to look into the hole, just like she was looking into the stream. But she leaned too far over, and in an instant, she was leaning too far and the weight of the unborn made her fall into the hole.

"She was free-falling, with no hope of reaching the bottom without a great crash. But as she descended farther and farther then, finally a great gaggle of many types of birds came to her and grabbed her clothes in their beaks. She was suspended in the middle of this flock, with nothing above her or below to grab onto except the great sea turtle lying there without a worry. She landed softly on his back, and as quickly as they had come to her aid, they again took to flight and were gone. The birds flew away in all directions, leaving her alone once again but on a firm spot.

"She still clutched some of the roots of the Great Tree, and she planted them in the cracks and folds of his giant shell. He did not mind. She prayed, and the place we call Turtle Island was created. It exists to this day.

"Then the woman who had fallen into the great hole from the sky had her child. It was a daughter. She was so beautiful the entire world as we know it began to sing."

As I look around the campfire, the children are so quiet not even the youngest has fallen asleep. It is a good time for us. The boys are now perched on their haunches and stare at Enita like they have never seen her before, and all is good in this village.

Enita continues. "The daughter is taught her mother's ways, and she joins in a union with the West Wind. She has two unborn children within her belly, who begin to quarrel even before they come out to the light. They fight about who will come first to emerge. The Left-Handed Twin refuses to come out the usual way. He decides to come out of his mother's armpit, and it kills her. The newborn children bury their mother right there, and she becomes known as the Corn

125

Mother. She holds all the seeds to the corn, squash, and beans in her hands. We know them as our Three Sisters from then on. From her heart grows the sacred tobacco. It is used to send messages and our thanks to those still in the sky world.

"The two brothers continue to compete with each other, and they begin to create all the animals of Turtle Island. Then they create the plants to feed them. This teaches them they are different. Right-Handed Twin creates the beautiful hills, all the lakes we see today, and the gentle spring blossoms. He created all the gentle creatures around us. But the Left-Handed Twin created the jagged cliffs, and the fierce whirlpools in his brother's lakes and streams. He created the thorns and all the predator animals that seek out the meek. Left-Handed Twin is so angry at Right-Handed Twin for creating human beings that they never talk again.

"Right-Handed Twin is known as our Creator. He is called the Master of Life. Left-Handed Twin helped with it all, but he created the rituals of sorcery and those of healing. He has a life in the shadows from the first day. The world they created included both cooperation and strong competition that still exists among us this day. They invented loving kindness, but they created hate and war and aggression to make it all even.

"When they finished, they still competed against each other, always trying to outdo the other's deeds. They began to gamble and learned our game of lacrosse, and then they invented the war club. One day not so long ago, Right-Handed Twin grasped an antler and killed his only brother, Left-Handed Twin. All were sad who witnessed it. Right-

Handed Twin throws his brother over the edge of this new world, and he claims the light of the day and gives his brother the world of the night and the lower world to rule, thinking this is a good thing for him to do.

"Their grandmother, Sky Woman, is so angry about the murder of one of her grandsons by Right-Handed Twin that she accuses him of the wrongdoing. He becomes angry with her, for he believes she always liked Left-Handed Twin better, and he cuts off her head and thrusts it skyward. It became that very moon we see over there."

Enita then points to the fullness of it and shows them the eyes, the mouth, and the nose of the grandmother, and a great moan carries over the entire circle. All who are there are looking skyward now, even the young bucks pretending not to listen to her. Some of these same boys are getting restless and begin to stir but are soon hushed by their mothers, and they return to their spots on the ground without any disrespect. More of our strong drink is handed around again, and they oblige us with cakes and the sweets we also prepared. It is a wonderful sight. I now know we are all a family once again.

In a moment, Enita, now refreshed, is standing as tall and straight as I have ever seen her. And she continues.

"He then threw her body into the ocean, and it creates all the fish and creatures of the sea. Oh, it's a wonderful time. It is our belief that we need the Left-Handed Twin and the Right-Handed Twin to show us the way we began. We need them to be in balance with our world. We feast, we sing, and best of all, we dance to honor the Left-Handed Twin. The day belongs to his brother alone, the

Right-Handed Twin. They will continue to struggle with each other for all time until time is no more, and we must know which brother to honor. We must learn to balance our needs against what is there for us to take. But we must never favor one over the other."

Enita quietly sits down from where she rose, and all of us there want to sit next to her. But little Kewani comes forth before there is even a hush, and she recites my little prayer word for word. She isn't shy and has no loss of voice. I think the men at their camp may be able to hear her. I, for one, hope it's so.

She begins.

> *Oh, Father above, I love you so.*
> *Oh, Mother Mary, I need you so.*
> *Oh, Mother, I miss you so.*
> *Oh, my brother, where did you go?*
> *I look for you all to guide me so.*
> *Come one and all, and hold my hand.*
> *Make me welcome here and in your land.*

We all bend to her last word, and then we again rise and dance along the fire's edge. It is a good night, and we will continue for a time. I, for one, am proud of my sisters and am happy to be a Mohawk.

What's that, Mother? Yes, I will hand you the cup. It's your turn to tell us a story.

The Longhouse was the center of the Mohawk Family living
arrangement A small village would have a few of these type of structures
as well as many smaller dwellings

Chapter VII
Into the Longhouses

Oh, Mother, I miss you so.

I am here now only with the help of my aunts and those of her family. It is not of my own accord. I look to the space you once occupied, and there is nothing left. All of your pots of clay and the one of the bright metals have now been given to others of the tribe to enjoy. Maybe that one special pot will be for the whole village to share? I hope this is so, as it was given to you by my father at your union before I was born. All of what was yours is now gone from this place we once called home. Even your finely made clothes that you worked so long to make by the light of the fire are gone. They have all been given to those who are much less skilled. All of your possessions have been passed around and have left this house. Your baskets full of treasures we all collected have been taken. Even the beads of glass with so many colors have a new hut to be displayed in. They have all vanished from right in front of me as if I didn't exist. Even that little basket that held them all so well was your first one, I'm told.

Little was offered for me to keep. I think it is because of my age, but I really don't know why. I only was allowed to keep the strung beads of wampum you made with the smooth shells, so beautiful in their coats of purple and white. I remember you making the cross fashioned from the birch. It is so fine to hold in my hand. I will never let it go, and it will never leave my hands.

I found the little book with the cover of buffalo skin given to you by those of the black robes. It was still in its hiding place, and no one else found it except for me. I had watched you place it there many moons ago, and it will remain there until we move on from these bows. It shall never be far from me. Yet I know not what the words say and have no one here to teach me, as they, too, have left us here alone. I need to hear those words again so I can repeat them as we did when we worked the fields and harvested the squash I so remember.

I can still hear your voice in its sweet and soft tone, reciting the words and prayers over and over again, but it is becoming so faint. I remember some of the words to the prayers that you said so often even though your voice was barely a whisper to us for fear of being discovered by Father or one of the elders. But we never were discovered by them, and you even sang your songs to us when he was with the men and enjoying his pipe, sitting right outside of this place. Even the shaman told us it was wrong and we should turn these men of the cloth away from our huts. But you held your ground so well, and they all turned to retreat, some shaking their heads as they walked away.

The chants you recited were so beautiful to us. They seemed as if quieted by the night air falling on them, but we heard you clearly enough. I can close my eyes and see you and still hear you this day as I heard you then, when you would draw us near to your bosom, but will it always be so? I will say the words you have taught me with a soft and mellow voice because this is how I will remember you. You were my mother, and there is not one woman here who will ever take your place even though some have tried. I thank them, but to me, you will never truly be gone.

I will hide the book under my own gown as you did and carry it with me at all times to protect it from them. It shall be as if it is part of me all my life as it was a part of yours. I will hide it from them, for they will frown upon it, and they may toss it upon the open flames of a cook fire just in spite. Or they may even place it in the ground for the worms to feed upon, for they told you this, and I have not forgotten their cruel words to torment you. It is now up to me to keep it safe and protect it with my life. It needs to come to this, for I shall never have another to learn from, and I keep it to keep your memory alive as well.

The brothers come fewer times now, and I must wait long days between their visits for them to return. The young seem to know they are near our village a long time before they break from the cover of the trees. But they come even knowing how my uncle feels about them, yet they say it is "God's will," not theirs, and I believe them. They have many to visit in other villages now, yet we seem to be on the early days of their trek this time. There are only three of them who show here without notice, and it will never be the same season that they appear again to us as it used to be. I am not sure if they are following the last of the snows to come this time, as it may now be the autumn before we see them again. They seem to enjoy coming while the men go for the pelts, when they do not have to discuss their intentions with them.

Their guides often flank them, but these Hurons are a weaker Indian, Father had once said. They bend to the wishes of these men of the Lord and do not speak their free will as we do. They come covered from head to foot in the blackness of their cloaks, with great brimmed hats upon their heads to shield them from our sun. Most are aged men and wise like our elders, yet the two never seem to sit down and speak to each other. I wonder why this is so?

Uncle Iowerano turns his back to them as soon as they appear and says they may not wander our village alone. He trusts them not, and he has a young man stand with them wherever they go. He has said they must sleep in the lodges and be attended by us at all times, but he has ordered us not to be alone with them without an aunt or maiden with us. But he does not prevent them from coming here, and he is the only one who can banish them. While other men shall complain, he remains silent. It is my chore to feed and carry water to them, and for this, I do not mind at all. It is the time when I can see them close at hand and say words that must remain silent when they are gone. It will be their eyes alone that will first see us as we awake each day.

We all kneel in prayer together in this tight space for most of it. I will ask them to teach me the marvelous ways of your book, Mother, and recite each page willingly, using my nights learning its meanings by the dull glow of the campfire. The Jesuits will leave us early today, we have just learned, but promise to return within a few days to continue our lessons. It seems there are Frenchmen encamped not far from here that they wish to see, and they do not want them to look for them here in our midst, especially since the hunting party has not returned. They promise to teach us more of their songs when they return, but I, for one, wish only to discover the meanings of this tiny book you hid from everyone except me.

Oh, Mother, I miss you so, but I have your charms, and I will learn your ways to keep you close. I love you, Mother, and all the things you held dear. I want to find you someday and walk the path to the Lord with you in sight. I want Brother to come along with us. I want to watch over him again so you can go to the fields and the stream without fear that he will be taken. I want to walk with the one you so adore, but best of all, I want to bring Father with us to meet the chief that even he will bow down to.

Oh, Mother, I wait for the day when your blessed Mary will come to me and I, too, will feel safe and warm. I lie here night upon night, never quite asleep, for I'm afraid I will miss you when you come to bring me home. How will you find me once we make the ride to the new place high above us and through the trees, hidden from all below except the smoke that swirls upward from the rings now new and clean, with a fire ready but not lit?

The morning is so long in coming, and the sun has yet to make its appearance, but we have been up and preparing for this day for some time now.

The clouds overhead seem to be racing each other through the darkness and are always replaced by new ones as they disappear. I will lie here on my back for a brief time more to catch all that is going on while I wait for the great kettle to come to a boil. It does not disturb me or bother my sight to gaze upward before the sun rises higher, for I am looking for the gates that are there for us to enter. I think I have seen them once, shining far above my head, but I am not sure. I look up through the branches of the giant oak that stands mighty below the new place. And it makes everything seem as if it's in a woven basket. I can see the images clearly as I lie here, but they are moving off to the distant places as fast as a new one appears.

The shapes of the giant fan caused by the oaks and willows being intertwined seem to frame the sky above me as I move my head side to side. There, I see so many animals, and over there, a tree and a canoa appear, but they are ever changing. It is a great sight, and I wonder what they must look like from the place of our Lord as he looks down upon all that is below him. Does he see the same things I do?

There is much motion outside this place this morn. I hear the adze and the chop of the axe, yet they are distant, and no wood has been piled for me to tote to our fire. There is smoke coming from the new place, as they have set many a tree to flame to shorten its length. The hills are shrouded in its grayness as if it was a fog, yet I know it is the workings of man, not the one you call a god. I have to explore this new place, but I cannot get there alone. I wait in patience for the men to return, but it has been a day or so, and this place is growing silent and cold. It is as I remember it the day you left. I have that same feeling about our home. It, too, is dying an awful death. Some of us from this house have gone there, and to return is surely in doubt. And where they once lay, there is nothing to claim—all has been taken. There is nothing left except the silence.

The braves have finally decided to return at the close of this day, and again I must go, for they are taking out the last of this hut's benches, and it is now bare to all who wish to enter, man or beast of the forest. We are finally preparing to move to the higher ground and never to return to this village. This night will be our last here, and I am so sad for it. Nothing is to be left but the memories and the soot that has stained the wood from the smoke's swirling dance to the ceiling of those many fires. We all watched as you read to us from your great book from right over there, but now I am alone here and cannot find your face in the clouds above me anymore, yet my search will continue until you appear again.

My dear uncle, Iowerano, who has claims to be our chief, has taken me into his family after you all left with the pox. He has told the women that I am now his daughter, and it is his wish that I shall be taught by them from this time forward. And I shall not be allowed to fall behind because of my sight or condition. I, for one, Mother, do not want to be treated differently, for I do not know anything but the hard work, as they call it. I, for one, call it love of another, and I will not fail in my chores. But to them, if I cannot keep pace and do my share, he will cast me out into the night as if I didn't exist. He should not worry so, for I am the daughter of the two who were the strongest of our kind, and I will honor you both by doing all in my power to thank him for this gesture.

Oh, it is a time of sadness for me but one of wonderment as well. I remember the time not so long ago when we were all happy together in this place. When we all could walk the paths down to the stream, I was running ahead and Brother was on his board, secured by your own loving hands as you tied the twine to keep him safe. Then the sickness came in the middle of the night to us and took over our daily lives. Your breath was stolen as if a fox had come from the wooded area and snatched it away.

Then the cough and all the pain that followed was brought to bear upon our flesh. Baby was the first to go in the sickness, and then Father was taken from us. He tried to get off the mat, yet it wasn't to be. I still can see him struggle as he looked up, first at me and then away, as if he had been beaten. A tear rolled down his face—the first and only one I ever saw. It told me of his pain of heart and body. He would talk of his childhood all the night long as he lay there, but it was you he called out for so often. And then he, too, fell silent and cold.

Finally, it was you to fall to its evil way. You, Mother, never complained, not once. You asked for forgiveness, but from what, we know not. I then watched from my pelts as the women came and knelt over you. The sisters of this longhouse tended your every need as you lay there so peacefully that we all held our own breath to see if you were still alive. It was a quiet time when you met the Maker, the Creator, or the one you call Lord. It was after the moon had begun its descent into the hills far behind us that you closed your eyes to never see us again.

Oh, Mother, I miss you so. I long for the time when we are all together again. Surely there is a place of the Curator that will house us all again. Father will again be chief of all he surveys, and you, my dearest Mother, will be there beside him, your face aglow as if it is the sun rising from its slumber. Those who now walk past this place and peer into its small room will again be those he governs over, but only when we are all gone. He was chosen to do so by the word of the elders and from the smoke of our ancestors. He was a great chief, and he knew compassion and fairness along with his swift justice dealt out to those he wished to punish. He led those many people of the Turtle Clan with the ability to know he had chosen his mate wisely. But best of all my memories, he was a good man to you and us as his children. He protected us and comforted us with all he had inside him. He trusted in you to teach us the ways of his people, although you were born of others from far away.

But we will be venturing away from this camp, my home, and the place of my birth. The land where you all lie silent in the ground will cease to exist soon, for we will move the village to the high place up the great river just about as far as I can see on this clearest of all days. The men have been there for some time, and some of the squaws have now departed to burn the trees and gather the logs together. The fields are to be sown upon the uncut meadows, and the water there, they say, is as clear as they have ever seen. It bubbles up from deep in Mother Earth as cool as the winter snow even on the driest of days of the time with the sun overhead.

It pools upon the soil in the shade of the hill. It is as sweet as the dew upon the petals of the prairie flowers in the dawn of the time.

Oh, I do not want to go, but what should I do? I cannot cut the alder or strip the bark. The seeds for the planting are not as dry as they should be, so I rake them often and will turn them once more. Then I will lay a blanket upon them to keep the moon from wetting them again. But it is not enough. I know I can do more. The braves have moved there now, except the few he has set as sentry. The elders come and go, and we have loaded the great canoas to the wales with the items we wish to keep. My longhouse is bare except for the robe placed in the corner where I will remain until they call me to go with them as well.

As I look at the bareness of it all, I see now for the first time how it came to be, with the bows bent way above me to form its shape. The bark of the woods is everywhere, yet not one insect has called it home. The trees were cut oh so long ago, before my birth and all that I know. They lashed it all with the hides of the elk tied tightly at all sections so the wind cannot blow us in.

The once-proud ring that held the great flames is now smoldering upon the soil. We will need it a few more times, but there are fewer of us, and we need not a grand torch in front of us. The stones will stay, as will the shards of the cook pots that broke under their own weight. We will make new ones from the soil of the river. We will roll the stones from the fields to make up the new rings to tender the fires and keep us all warm and safe.

Down have come the platforms, and some lie just outside, as the others have already been carted away to be used again. I know this place in my dim sight, but it is changing, and it will be strange for me to find my way without the post and beams to guide me on my way. They have taken the shelves that held our stores and removed them together and brought them on the journey to this new place. They have taken the doors, one at each end, but have left the hatches in the top to let out the smoke. Perhaps tomorrow they will go away as well. They say they are better than the ones they could build new, and to make some of the new place from some of the old house will invite the spirits to come with them. I hope they bring you to me in the nights when it is cold so I can see your loving face, and that will melt the snow above us and bring the time of plantings again.

I see you again in this light of the fire, Mother. You are always smiling at me and tending the boy child. He is there with you as well, for Father again will lift him upon high when he, too, joins you. And all will rejoice in the knowledge that you will be together in this place of many of our ancestors. I am not sad this day, but I know not what is expected of me, being the youngest of the women who live in the longhouse of my aunt, and there must be a purpose.

As I walk to the edges of the village, I can touch its fence, and it feels familiar in shape to me. A lone dog is scampering around, yelping as if expecting another of his kind to reply. The air is silent, however. The fire in the center, too, has gone cold. There have been flames heating the night since I came to stay here, and for them not to show against the sky is chilling to me, as if it is a symbol of the day that hasn't come. I cannot walk the great distance unescorted, but maybe I should head toward the wondrous noises coming from the hill far away. There is no drum or flutes to follow, just the din of the chopper's axe. The air hangs thick with the smoke of their fires. I think maybe I will stay here alone and call on you to visit me again. This is home, and I will not forget it.

Another night, I stay on the floor. There is no raised bed for me again. It, too, has been claimed. I do not wish to cause a concern, but the earth clings to all it touches. The dampness is in my bones, and my head is not as clear. Yet I will lie here a moment more, not out of anything to fear but for I know it has come close to the time when I must be carried away from here too. The men have carted off the last of all they can save to the new place.

A few others and I are called upon to bring down the blankets and the emblem of the Turtle Clan from the front of the lodge. Father put it there so long ago, but now it has been brought to the ground and handed to me to carry. I hold his memory with honor as we trudge to the edge of the soil and strike out down the deeply grooved path to the shore.

It is odd that there are so many canoas here because there doesn't seem to be enough men to paddle them the distance to the new place. Some are turned up like a turtle and surely will not be brought with us. Then a few of them are pulled up into the sweetgrass and turned over as if to keep them safe. Some have been here for a long while, and then I see my father's war canoe. No one has used it since he met the Creator. And I am told it will stay behind and not be towed to the shore above us. It makes me remember him all the more, for I used to watch him and my uncle spirit off on some exploration or to head downstream to block the waters and bring home a bounty of fish. I used to sit in the bottom of it, not being able to see over the sides but looking straight up and watching the clouds in the sky. It was a magical time, and I loved it so. I will always think of the times we had, and the image of it almost riding in the grass makes him all the closer to me, yet I, too, am sad that we cannot ride down to the great water together until I find him and we all go to Mother's heaven.

We are to be loaded into the remaining canoas with the cages of the last of the birds, the old dog, and whatever else they can tote. I cannot see the passage, but it will not prevent me from feeling the river below me as we move along, one with it.

The ride is rather a short one and is quickly done, but I still cannot find the place we all shall call home, for it is hidden well up the hills in front of me. We have pulled into the head of a swift stream that enters our river, but we cannot go farther unless we do it on foot. The current is so strong, and there appear to be many rocks protecting its fall from the hill above. I am led partway up through the alders, and then I can see a new cut. The trees have all been cut and burned to allow a trail as wide as I ever have seen to be formed. It shall be our new path, I'm told, and one we can defend against the French should they come in the night to burn down our huts and scatter us into the hither land. I see the shapes of outlying huts and lean-tos and the makings of a field or two, yet not one stalk of corn has been planted or a row of squash been seeded. I believe this shall be my work, for I can make it grow. I ask to be pointed to the spring they claim as pure and clear, and after a great trek, I am there too. It is so beautiful here, high in the freshness of it all.

The castle is a good place. I can feel this in my bones. It is a safe place that will be a new beginning for all of us, for there is no sickness here to claim us.

The long distance from our river will give them the time to gather the men if a raiding party should be seen below us. The newly built walls will be of a great defense to us should we need them to hold them back. It is so sad to me that our once-proud-and-thriving nation is reduced to just a few longhouses now. There will be no more than a dozen or so. Where there were once nearly one hundred or so spreading out from the old village, there no longer is the need for them. All are built inside the walls, for without the protection of those thick timbers, we may all pass the way of those gone before us, and who would catch sign of us if we all are gone? We must keep all that may come to harm us at bay, and here, I do feel safe and at peace.

Oh, Father, if this were your village, you would make it so grand. Like you, it would stand so tall that the great oaks and the meadows around its summit would be overrun with children—the children you always called the life of us all. Without them, there is no hope, is there? Yet here we are, now so few. Are we to go away like you did and leave little behind?

The waters of the spring bound from Mother Earth's green cloak with no assistance from us at all. It falls downward untethered above its banks on a path to the river behind this new place. We are now and forever surrounded by life's water, it seems. It swells and rises as it passes to our river, and everything it touches along its voyage of the earth flourishes. Even when the rains of the planting time or the snow after winter's sleep come down her bed, all she touches, from your mighty oaks to the grasses, stands taller for touching her. What a beautiful sound she makes as she rambles down the face of one hill and through another until it grows silent again and passes the old place.

Oh, Father, I miss you so. This would be a splendid place if you and Mother could join me here. Brother would grow as swift and tall as the corn if he, too, had only survived the white disease. I'm here alone among all those who are left. Few of us will build outside these walls, yet many will come within to trade inside them. Some even find this place and return to its protection. It is a good place.

Even the black robes will return to send us the word. My uncle does not want them here, and he turns his backside to them when their canoas glide by. But he has said they can come and build their chapel, but by their own hands. He has said the captured can be only the ones they sermon. These tribesmen of another village, too, go without food for the day they will not work. Some are beaten or tortured for it, but only the words of Mary are heard from them. None has screamed or passed under the pain, and all of them show up in the morning sun, ready to have it happen again. I wonder what drives men to honor her so.

Mother, if she were here, could guide me even more. There is a lot to learn and so much I do not know. They are our horses and pull our plow, but they are fathers and brothers, and some must have a mate. I feel sorry for them sometimes, but it is, after all, our way. The men of Christ will come and build their own longhouse here. We have been told by the chief not to assist or interfere. They will portage all their own food and want. I'm not to gather berries or nuts or bring a bag of water, for they are not here to us—at least that is what I'm told. I hear the chants, and it draws me nearer. I know these psalms. They are the same you whispered so clear to us when I was a child. They have stayed with me forever like the image of your face. I will never forget any of it until we are all again in one place.

I can feel the bark of the fence under my hand as I pass by and rub against its coarse skin. I must get my senses about me in this new place, for if I wander too far off, I will be lost forever. Even the squat dog of the old place has made the journey here. I think I will bring him to the spring tomorrow and bathe him in its waters. For now, I will walk with him and share my food, but he is one I fear will light off at the first sign of someone else's cook fire. For now, I will share the lodge, and he will always be welcome. He and I are alone, it seems, in a place of others.

I can find the hut, and I will enter through its familiar door, yet it, too, has grown smaller and not as tall. They are the same, I believe, we had in the old place, which you fashioned of the woven twigs. I like to touch it and remember when it was ours. I am not sad at the feel, for it, too, brings the images of you all, and I know I will be safe to lie upon this floor and drift off to sleep. We are together here at last. You have found me, and I am thankful for this. I will bring the beads and stay on my knees, praying throughout this night, thanking him for making us welcome.

Our home of my dear mother had many of our kin. This one will house just the a few families that are left on this earth. We must look to the future and not so much to the past. It is a good structure, built so tight, but there is no place that the fire ring will be able to let us do its dance. How will the smoke rise on its own and find its way to the sky? I must tell them tomorrow to make this thing right or I will never see the faces as the embers take to flight. But that is for tomorrow. This night, I must take up my prayers and feel the beads through my hands. This comforts me, and I am beginning to understand I am not here for just the chores of the day. I am here to spread your word, Lord, and on earth I must stay until I can walk the path to those gates far above, and you will be there with a smile and your arms opened wide to invite me in. Oh, what a special day that will be, and I must begin to prepare.

I will adorn these walls with the lilies I can find. Their whiteness will bring a touch of the quiet forest floor into this darkened place. They will search for the sun that is just outside, and I will make the blossom as long as I can. There will be many crosses I've fashioned from willow and larch. The quills will grace a special place, and I will work at making this a familiar home. There is so much to do.

Your pots are here. I can see them now. They look so good on the benches near the ring, yet they are filled to the rim by the others' hands that got to keep them for their own. I welcome them to share them, for to see they are well used reminds me of you. I am not sad at this and find you where I care to look. Your sisters have taken me into their place, and for this, I am thankful. Our family all have tiny pieces of you to share, and I see you in my dreams. Oh, Mother, I love you so but know you are near me at every glance—a box full of beads, a basket made so fine of the sweetgrasses woven in our fashion. Oh, Mother, I can clearly see you now, sitting by the fireside, ready to read from the book. I have kept it safe from harm and wait for the time when I can return it to you. I hide it often in our special place, but I must take it and feel its leather, for it warms me with the touch. I say the Hail Mary many times a day, yet she has come to me but once, and I wish to talk with her again. I will have no fear. I want to ask her how you are doing and if I will be coming home soon to see you in her place.

The smell around me is of the new and wet woods. They stripped the thick bark to make the planks and covered its long, high sides to keep out the snows. They bent the tallest of the freshest bows that now cover us all so well. It is like a giant basket that holds people instead of our corn. The weather shall not enter here, for they have made the chief proud. It is a fine house, and all are welcome here should anyone care to enter. I will hang my father's sign outside the opening for all to see. It is a proud symbol of our ancestors and will make our house of the Turtle Clan finally finished. It is a good sign, and it tells all who enter here they are protected, and all will be welcome.

As you enter, it smells so sweet and not of the smoke or cook pot, but it will in time. I believe it will become familiar as time goes by. It is not yet a house lived in, and to me, it still is just a shell. We will fashion the eves with bows and herbs. We will dry our maize high up to keep it well. We will raise the cages out of the smoke, and once we hear the birth of the children, then and only then will I call it home.

I have hung the snowshoes my uncle has fashioned for me. They will make it easy to fetch the water in the snow. I thank him for his gifts, and he brings out a newly carved pipe. He said it was for my father, but he had never finished it before he was gone. I see him move silently away as if the bees in our field have stung him. I thank him for this wonderful gift. I will honor him from now on. He, too, has become my father.

The sun is moving over the hills, and I see the wind is bending the tallest of the great trees. It is an eerie feeling among this place when the day draws to a close. I no longer feel as safe. At night, I sense the demons come and dance across the sky, looking for our new homes and us. Yet I can call to Mary as often as I may, and she will have them sent away time and again.

I look to the heavens and can see the gates now clear. It won't be long before I, too, take that trip, and once I start upon that journey, I will call out to you to come fetch me, and I will call out her name, for she will take my hand and guide me the rest of the way.

The longhouse is warm, yet no fire has been set to burn. We are now here together. The new garden is outside my door. I will begin tending it tomorrow to bring it along. I will cart the water from the spring in the morning light. I shall prepare a meal, if not a feast, for all who have worked so hard. But before I do, I must go to the ground and pray for all we have received and look again into the face of the children to carry on the words my mother so gracefully spoke in our village, now hidden in the woods.

Tonight, we all will dance around the great flames, and it will be a joyous occasion as we all eat and beat the drums in thanksgiving. It may last a few days, I'm told. I have not seen such an affair myself, but the older squaws say they have moved many times. Ossernenon was a longtime place, and they are happy to move on.

We are in a great fervor when the warriors return from the river below. They have set the old village to the torch, and a glow appears over the trees. They have been drinking the spirits of the whites and are acting very odd. They are falling down like the ducks that eat the fermented fruit of the elderberry. I do not wish to witness this anymore. I want to go to my house and pull the flap of beaver over its thatched door. But my uncle forbids this, and I must not shame him, so I will sit in silent prayer till they all are quiet again. I will not show them I fear their ways, for it has been told to me that they will stone those who are not like them.

I, for one, was born among them. I am not a captured slave to be treated in such a manner. I raise my eyes skyward and say the words you taught. The smoke from my village is carrying away its spirits as the embers reach where the clouds used to be. I see that the fire below has taken a giant step, and the earth shall cry tomorrow, for it shall be scorched as never before. It has come to the river's edge, and the water runs black with its fill of it.

I think of my father's canoa, as it must have been consumed too. Oh, they have erased all traces of them except those of my own mind. When will I get to travel there and pick through the soot? I believe we have taken everything we could, but I need one more look to find anything of my mother that I could hold still dear. Oh, Mother, it is a frightful thing to see how the flames grow. Will it move across this place and consume us here as well?

Can you see it from your new home? It must be quite a sight! I wish I were beside you to watch the colors and see all that light. But if you should ever miss me, I'm right there to find. Just look to the tall hill with the crosses that abound. I have marked your way to find me well, and I wait almost in silence. My handiwork is all you have to see, and just ask for me. And I will be willing to come. I'm here, dearest Mother, and here I shall wait until you send me the directions. Only then we shall see the trail as you have spoken of it. It is to me a mere fact. It is not of the smoke, for I have seen it as clear as the stones in the stream. I have never really moved here, and I have yet to unpack. I have all that I need and am waiting with your book wrapped in black and the shells of the distant waters grasped tightly in my fist. If you come for me this evening, I promise not to resist. I am ready to join you, and I welcome you to our new home. Just come to me, Mother, and I will recognize you and will make you comfortable. This, too, is your place.

Kanawauke (Great Waters)

Chapter VIII
The Long Journey Home

Under the cloak of the pitch blackness of the moonless night, they slipped silently out of the protection that the longhouse had afforded them. Quickly they were absorbed by the dark as they rambled down the wooded hill, through the alders, the yellow birch, and the tall white oaks all standing sentry in front of them.

They are traveling swiftly to reach the banks of the river far below them. Moving as one, they leave little to no sign on the ground behind them, certainly nothing that could be followed, even by the best of the native trackers. Their feet are light and sure, nary a branch disturbed as they gain speed on the steep incline ever forcing them forward. Now they are all swallowed by the trees as they move toward the hidden canoes and simply cease to exist.

There are many in this party, but unlike the hunting groups from Caughnawaga that have been coming and going from the village for the past two days, they are of a different purpose. These twelve men and the lone precious child are heading for the big water to the north and are running contrary to the wishes of the chief and his shamans. For now, they are well under the protection of her ancestors and the cover of the night—not even the great owl is disturbed by the intruding clutch.

The Mohawk elders wanted her stoned. The never-ending threats to put her to death were growing more and more vocal as they came to fear her mysterious ways and her constant chants, which they all refused to make familiar. She was forbidden to speak of her god, Rawanniio.

The only men of the village left behind to offer any defense at all were the very young who could not yet leave their mothers' sides, still carrying sticks to fend off enemies of the night, or the very old who were gray and feeble, their teeth worn to nothing more than a nub or two so that chewing of the flesh is now just a memory to them. Death will surely come to many of these once-proud braves before the melt of next winter's snow runs into the streams and pools again, before it finally winds its way to the great water far away to the east.

None would be of much resistance to those now spiriting Tekakwitha away from the home of Tsaniton-gowa and Kahontake, her parents, and her young brother, all laid to rest in shallow graves just outside her shared longhouse. She knows she will never be able to return here, yet she does not look back, for she can see the village clearly through her closed eyes and not those she has peered through these many years now.

All the strong boys yet to go on their first vision quest and the seasoned hunters alike have descended on the upper river valleys in the hunt for the now-elusive bear and deer. Some come back to their hunting camp after a long day carrying a few rabbits clinging to their belts and nothing more. They are sure the hunt will extend a few more days, and it's the runners' notice from the camp that has finally set Father Lamberville's plan into its final stages. They will not have another chance like this one until the planting moon or even when the winter snows begin to fall from the sky. No, if there is to be an escape to Sault Sainte Marie, in the hopes this precious child can be saved from her own kind, they must leave this night, well before a hint of new day is in the air.

She comes away willingly, of her own accord, without much more than a smile on her face. She has been scorned and beaten and threatened even by the youngest of those people from her adoptive village. She does not fear their wrath yet takes it as a sort of penance. She has often held her ground against even the strongest of the young bucks, their bulk seemingly swallowing her petite image as they stood in front of her, sometimes threatening to pummel her with a stone placed in each hand, but it was always her image that cast the tallest of shadows. Many of them left almost skulking away from her presence, and they never challenged her twice, for they knew better of it.

She is a willing student of the Jesuits and, because of her faith, now is an outcast. Her uncle cannot protect her anymore. Beloved Kateri will leave the sign of the cross on many a birch sapling in hopes the natives will take it as a good omen, yet they, in turn, will peel each one from the trunks as if they fear them. Each one, however, will leave a permanent scar upon the tree that reminds the young maidens of the village where she once walked. All of this then brings to mind an image of her face so deeply pitted and swollen red by the disfigurement of her youth, one image many of the children grew to fear, while still others were brought to tears by seeing it.

Some, a precious few, never saw the marks at all and believed she was so beautiful to behold. They will silently mouth the prayers she taught them, and they, too, rub the beads that Kateri has made for them with her own hands. But it was the care and unselfish manner she undertook everything with that made her stand out to them. For many of them, they saw the beauty and purity of her very being, and more will follow her north when they, too, proclaim their faith. But today they weep in solemn silence, for she has moved on, and they still fear for her very life. They will go to her longhouse looking for her, but now it is nearly empty.

Father Lamberville is there but quite alone. He, too, is ready to leave of his own accord, but he will not travel with her this day. His age prevents him taking a swift route, and he must first travel along his circuit to preach the word to still more of the children of the woods. He hopes eternally to find a lily of the Mohawks again among the thorns of the brambles that block his forward passage each and every day he awakes. He is resolute; however, he has done the righteous thing. He has liberated her, he feels, from the stone and branch that will nevermore strike her precious flesh. He has fallen to his knees as he spies the eyes of these children upon him now, for he knows she touched their souls as she reached his. And they all will be better for the brief time she was among them.

Many wear the beaded robes and moccasins she crafted in the dim light of her hut, for she would not stand in the sun for long before her eyes would fail her altogether. The fine stitches were as tight and strong as any they had ever seen, since her hands touched them like no other. Not another maiden of the forest could ever hope to replace her work with theirs, let alone match its beauty. No finer wears will ever be found among the squaws of the Mohawk Tribe of the Turtle Clan.

She was always at peace in the darkness, and tonight was to be no different to her. She never felt she was truly alone, for she always had her prayers and her mother to reach out to and hold close to her. In the privacy of her dwelling, she was loved and appreciated, yet should she step out, those who once praised her would easily raise a switch or stone to her, for it was the way of the native. Yet it is the grace she showed in her daily chores that caused them to follow behind her, ever so silent but always listening. Now they have grown and will say the words she has taught them, and they will pass along her prayers to those still laced to the boards or those still clinging to the teat, for she has brought the word of the Lord to them, and it has taken root. And her tribe was not willing to allow her this right, for it wasn't their way. The whites are not mentioned in the spirit world of the drum and flute, and cannot lead them to anything but the sickness or the liquor that crazes them.

The five great war canoes are nearly lifted out of the water with each stroke of the paddles. They are lunging forward as if in a race amongst themselves, but each man so tall and thick of muscle knows they are in a different sort of contest. They are here to liberate her and spirit her away out of harm's way. As if a magical event is occurring, they glide forward swiftly, covering miles of twists and turns as the river begins to dig deeper into the banks as they pass by, and now they are working the gorge with walls as high as any have ever seen before. They are plunging down the gorge as if descending the steepest of hills. Yet they are unafraid, for they know she will protect them, and she leads them in prayer as they push onward. Not one stroke falters, and all they leave behind is the swirl of the paddle as it trails off behind them in their wake. That, too, quickly disappears without so much as a telltale trace that man has been here before.

No, they will not be easy prey, but they are cautious and ever wary. The maiden Kateri Tekakwitha is on an odyssey of her faith, and she is alive this day with the excitement of the adventure. She is almost invisible, barely able to peer over the gunwale of the craft. She has been laid upon the skins of bear and elk, piled high to cushion her fragile frame and to insulate her from the bone-chilling cold of the river's water.

She anticipates a place where she will be welcome and will never feel the scorn, or another stone pelting her. She fingers the beads of her mother as they glide onward. Now even her prayers that she has said so many times to herself are being repeated by these men around her. They have been taught them well. This event is something she was not prepared for, but without opening her eyes, she bows her head down, and the music of the repartition echoes off the mighty stone walls as if a choir of hundreds is singing the praises of her blessed Mary.

As they reach the rapids, the canoa pitches and rolls. The birch-and-willow craft falls off one mound of water and is quickly swallowed up in the dark holes that lie in front of them, only to be pitched upward like a seed being spat out of a child's mouth. There is no fear on her face, however, just the constant look of an amazed child full of anticipation and excitement. She has placed her lot with the Lord, and she is comfortable in the belief he will deliver her through this great ordeal. She knows her purpose in life is to serve him, and she is calm and satisfied that she is now on her way to meet him.

These giants of her race press the paddles against the sides of the canoa, and it almost bends in two as it changes its course, slipping by the boulders rising up out to the turbulence in front of them. Not once do they let her be jolted by anything, for they are experts in everything they undertake. They were first chosen for the devout beliefs, yet being a skilled boatman and a fierce warrior was something they all would be required to possess. They will lay their lives on the line to protect her, and each knows their mission must not fail. To the man, they volunteered to deliver her, and to a man, they will willingly stand and face all who pursue her if necessary. And to a man, they will shield her from any and all harm, for they have come to bring her to her new home, one she will be strangely familiar with.

She now raises her head skyward and gives thanks for them. And they are humbled in her presence and silenced with her by her praise for them. They already believe she is a holy woman and divinely inspired, and they will not falter on their mission to protect her from all encounters and deliver her healthy and with great dispatch to the site just below the walled city known as Quebec, sitting on the pinnacle of the hills, not yet visible to her, not even in her imagination. She goes unafraid, with great anticipation of being yet closer to those who went before her and to finally be in the presence someday of her true father.

This task will test them all, for their enemy now has been alerted to the disappearances of her and the good Jesuit the same evening. They are indeed being followed, and they are running the banks on foot and through the woods as well as using the smaller swift-moving canoa. If they do not continue to move along, it will be a short time for them to be overtaken.

Her scars are deep this day as the sun begins to give her face a glow of the fire embers. She has pulled back her wrap and exposes her eyes and face to its warmth. No longer will she remain hidden from their view. She wants them all to see her as her Lord has made her. She is not ashamed of her look, yet she is mindful that others will stare at her. She is in hopes that they will see through the blemishes and discover her true inner beauty. The men of the canoa have already seen her, and they, too, believe she is radiant and wonderful to behold. It is their honor to transport her to her destination.

No more was the pox of her youth the subject of ridicule and torment. Finally, she is on her way home. That plague more than fifteen years ago made her heart heavy and weakened her body, yet it strengthened her resolve, and as she runs those tiny worn fingers over her mother's shells now crumbling to her touch, they are fortified by the ones given her by Father Lamberville, now interwoven with the words so often carried on her lips. She for once speaks aloud, and it sends a shiver throughout the men as if it were a startling war cry of an attacking enemy.

"Oh, Lord," she prays, "deliver us from evil."

The echo of her words resonates up and down the canyon walls, so much so that these brave escorts turn in unison to make sure no one is following their canoes, and some keep looking back over and over again to make sure once and for all. She is sure the man it was meant for has finally heard her prayer from her lips this day, and she is good with the world at last. Her heart has been lifted skyward, and no longer will she hide beneath a cloak to ease others' pain.

As they come around a bend in the river, the water slows. They are in the calm waters again. The men all breathe a sigh of uneasy relief, for they know their pursuers oh too well. She speaks to them first in her native tongue and then in French, and all are fixated on her face. She has risen from the skins and points a thin finger to the shore on the far side of the river now, and they paddle onward toward its banks and come into the shallows now teeming with speckled fish gliding just below the surface.

As the bow of the war craft slides up the white sands, the braves have already stepped ashore and raise the vessel up out of the water as she remains upright and does not waver or sway, and she is deposited far up the shore. Then another canoe, and still another, rides in their wake until all five have safely made it through the rapids and to a man. They sit on the sweetgrass of the riverbank, and to a man, they search the water they have just run for signs of those who pursue. This is an eerie place, almost sacred to them, for it is the same place where many of their ancestors have landed and made camp after a trek of many miles. Yet this is not the resting place. This will be a short respite from the waters of the river, but not one lean-to or skin will be stretched over the branches, for they must be wary of the complacent ways the slack water tends to bring to them.

No, they must take nourishment and then push on throughout the night. They have miles to travel, and to outdistance those of her village coming to do her harm, they must exhaust them and then replenish their minds with the spirit that she brings them to a man. She, though, goes to the birches and scribes another cross in the soft flesh of a strong sapling, just above her eye level, another telltale sign she has passed by this way. She does this unnoticed by those of the paddle, for they lie with the sun in their faces and eyes shut tightly, making the best of a few moments almost to a man, seemingly as if they are fast asleep. Yet they are not, and a noise of a boulder waking the bottom of the stream above brings them all to grasp their bow and spear. It is a false alarm, and the commotion doesn't even raise a look from Kateri as she kneels in prayer.

Soon the twelve natives again surround her as if to shield her from the view of the open waters. One by one, they slowly return to the boats, and so very soon they erase all signs they were there at all. The last acts are to place a small deserted robin's nest in front of the cross and then smooth the sand by raking it with a pine bow as the last man steps into his canoa. There is a slight breeze as they gain the center of the swollen pond, and it raises the hair on the neck of more than one.

The swifter and lighter canoas, too, have hauled out just above the rapids, waiting to rest themselves before they run through the high-stacked water full of boulders, and the thoughts of death are close to each of them, for none has been here before and the water seems extremely angry with them.

Kateri and her small flotilla reach the bend in the river, where they again put in. Here, it is decided that she must go overland, beginning far upstream from the fork where the big water begins. It is decided for her, and she leaves behind the five canoas and eight of her guard. The second night has passed, and she now is well inland from the portage, flanked by a very talkative Veda, who quietly wants to know all about her life. Then, there on her left is perhaps the largest of native couriers, Matanga, with the brothers Ajeeti and Akaash lagging behind them as if they are searching for any signs of others following, for they are. The porcupine path is deep and wide. Surely they will be upon him soon. Then they will walk on toe amongst the stones leading up to the top of the hill and the thinning trees. It all has been an uphill journey for them, sometimes slowing them to a crawl, arched over to prevent them from falling back, but they all seem to be walking a brisk pace. Even Kateri has not been tired by her ordeal, for she knows this is a righteous voyage.

The crisp evening air refreshes them as the night sky opens, with one bolide after another giving off the aurora of a great festival fire, and the streaking tails seem to come touch the earth just out of her reach. They have finally mounted the summit, and now they finally will rest for more than a few brief minutes. No fires will be set, but no one seems to care, as they are fast asleep—all except Kateri, that is. She continues deep in prayer, and a heavy-lidded Matanga sits motionless just outside her view. He fights the night with every measure of his frame until she finally lies down upon the robe they set out for her. Then he, too, is right with the world.

The five canoas are heading downstream and have reached the great divide where the one river becomes two, and three crafts go immediately to follow the larger stream while the remaining two are heavy in the water, with all the weight of the supplies shifted to them. But there is a reason for this. The faster canoas of her uncle's village are closing the gap and should be upon them by this time tomorrow. Chief Iowerano has demanded his braves go swiftly and dispatch those traitors and leave them where they lie. He has demanded this of them, and to a man, they will not end the search for the fair maiden Kateri until they have either killed them all or fallen in the attempt. By splitting them into two small parties, they hope that her ruse of going cross-country with the four strongest of men will protect her.

But they must eventually stop to sleep and eat, and if they are set upon in this darkness, they will not have an easy time of it. But they, too, lift their heads toward the falling stars, and she comes immediately to mind. They know now they have made her getaway by the river a good choice, and as they slowly paddle into the logan that washes back against the shore, two swift canoas go racing by and the advantage is theirs. They will sit here for this evening with the sound of the frogs and the hum of the insects. To some of the group, they are worse than the arrow and blade they just avoided. But night tends to calm even these warriors, and soon they stretch the paddles across the gunwales, and before they fall fast asleep upon them, the sound of their prayers breaks the silence, and even muted, the words carry from boat to boat. They pray for the tiny Kateri, now high on the hills with their best surrounding her, and with that thought, the last "ah-men" silences them all. Tomorrow they will need to avoid their pursuers and find a safe place to portage the canoas. In order to avoid them, they must cut inland and rejoin their kind.

Chapter IX
From the Hills of Sault Sainte Marie

Oh, Mother, help me so!

We have been here for some time now. The planting moon has risen and fallen since we first set foot here. But things are not the way they said they would be. I am sitting on the crest of this lowly hill yet still outside the Frenchmen's walled city. Why is this so? Are not we all from one Creator, or have they told me their lies to get me here to do their workings? I don't think the good Father Lamberville would lie to me or anyone else, but I have to know for sure. I'm their equal in Christ's eyes. He has told us this often enough. Yet here I am, sitting on the outside of their great fence, looking up from a very cold mound of their earth. Why is this so?

Why are we not within its walls? Do not we deserve to be safe from harm of a native attack or a scavenging bear? Why are these same children left out to fend for themselves as their mothers toil in the fields? Why are we to build our lean-to or wigwams of the forest out on the flatland below their city? I was told it was a great new village of much mud and stone that I was coming to. I have forsaken almost all my native beliefs to come here, and I have little in the way of remorse. I left without my aunts or my uncle's blessing, and he surely feels I have disgraced them and will not be forgiven. I am dead to him and his dear, sweet wife, Karitha. My life of seeking the Christian way was a constant source of trouble to them, and my belief in Mary almost cost me my wretched life as well. I will not accept the plight of one village to move on to one with the same lot. I, for one, feel we have been told an untruth, for it is not what they promised. Why is this so?

These small children who run past me don't seem to mind this place with its beautiful vistas and rolling fields of the yellow corn, but it really isn't much of a village for them to be reared in. I suspect they have many places to explore and new and wonderful adventures to claim, as they are constantly whishing by. They seem happy enough to be here, though I cannot imagine the way they felt to be forced to come here. In fact, they are constantly smiling as they ring me with their presence. They do not run away as others have. I believe there is some good being done here, but what will happen as they grow old? Will they still be forced to remain here, or will they be allowed to roam as our ancestors did?

They are being taught well of the Frenchmen's ways by the women of the robes who live only here. They have learned their lessons well and can talk of the Lord as well as any of the Jesuits. They do not venture too far from their fort, or they never will travel at night, and seldom will they go it alone.

I don't think they trust us. Some of them seem to enjoy being here. Many of these women always have a worried look about them. Others will school us but turn their noses upward as if they don't think we are worthy. They have come from across the great water and would not leave here at any cost to return to from whence they came, because of the terrifying journey. A few have told me they are worried that if they must travel back to their villages, it would be the death of them, and I have heard there was surely great suffering to them in the travels of their great canoes. They tell me they sailed in their great ship for more time than it took me to come all the way from Kahnawake

They brought the new prayers with them and a box of Bibles to give each of the children their own. There does seem to be more children here than Bibles again this season, and this is a good thing, for Father would be smiling if he knew we were again growing by the child. Their beads of their rosary are made of the colored glass and do not string well. Yet we can make do with them despite their tiny size. Their material for their robes is dark and lacks the colors of the traders' broadcloth we know so well. It is always the same and of little value when the winds blow. I can fashion a gown for those who have none that should make them pass through the doors to their school. I doubt if it will hold up long with the way it has been loosely woven. We really have no other choice, for they refuse us entry in our buckskins and beads. They say God does not like a woman who has to show her skin. I, for one, doubt he cares about this much at all, for he is about saving souls, and they have taught me a soul cannot be seen. I, for one, feel he will allow entry into his home regardless of what we are covered in as long as we are prepared to meet him.

They do not allow the children to play as I think they should. The nuns would rather they study their book and have lessons in their ways, not ours, and we are always scolded for our beliefs. They have come here to change us and make us in their image, it seems, not in his. I believe he is a god who believes in each of us as we are this day, not in how we can be changed to fit their image, isn't he? I so wish to live among them to learn more about the Lord. Are they more faithful than I? But I cannot live with the treatment of us as natives, for we have been here for a thousand years. Is there a special place in heaven for us outside the gates too? Are we to arrive at them only to be told we must set up our camp along its hills but not block the way for others like them?

Why is it, then, that we tend these crops for them, yet they go in through the great doors and beyond and leave us to our wigwams in the cold? Little comes to us once the harvest has begun. Our men still must venture out into the woods to hunt while they continue to sleep and wait for others to bring them their meal. I, for one, feel a person should reap what they sow as I have been taught by the Jesuits. I will make sure the children are fed, body and soul, as the scriptures tell us we must do. Are we just free labor? They needed, and they sent out the black robes to trick us into believing it was all for an inner peace? How am I going to return to the village of my people and tell them I have been tricked?

My uncle, Chief Iowerano, will not take this news lightly, and he will bring all the braves to a fever pitch with the drums and the smoke of the ceremonial fires. He will feed them the drink that will boil the blood in their veins and make them want to run through the forest all the way here. They cannot surely make siege to this walled city without great loss of life, yet he may just try to gain their trust and die in the attempt to enter as their equals. He will not allow me to ever again enter his village though, for I no longer exist to him. He will make me dead if I should come to the longhouses ever again. I am not afraid of this. I will live again in heaven. I have been taught this, and I, for one, cannot wait to join my mother and father.

It has been so many years since my brother has come to me that his image is no longer fresh to me. I miss them all so. I have prayed to Mary and her son to bring me home to them. I miss my people, yet they can come here freely now. The French king has killed many of my kind and changed us forever. The soldiers came with their muskets and torches and scattered those who remained throughout the woods and across the great rivers. Where does it all end? Do we all have to meet the Maker before we can truly be free of it all? I have chosen this life, and I have no regret. I am asking these questions so I can see the true reason for me to be here and will continue to question the things that I do not understand, for how will it be clear to me if I know so little?

The clouds are again moving swiftly over my head. They seem to be swirling a bit, and the faces they make are not clear to me. Brother wind is bending the branches that are singing in the pines, and I feel the cold chill of autumn coming to my flesh. It is coming early. Oh, I am so alone, yet I am among people like me. I have no family members here, and I am shuffled away from the events that draw me in close. The nuns' constant chanting is beautiful to me, yet I cannot sit with them. Why? The Jesuits say they are not for me to attend, for there is much drink and roasting of swine going on and it is not the way of the followers of the teachings of the black book, but they seem to enjoy these times, as do the others. I am told that I must repent to gain the gates of heaven, yet I go to bent knees many times each and every day but am not allowed to even enter the city they have built on our earth? What great event must take place for me to be worthy of them opening the gates of heaven for this poor native girl? Have they deceived me so? For what purpose have I remained alive while my kind have all gone before me?

The brothers say I have been chosen to spread the words they know so well. But I am here only to learn their words and say their prayers over and over again. I must learn their meanings, for some are distant to me, and it is hard for me to understand. What good does it do to say them aloud if we do not understand what they mean to us? We recite the simple prayers to Mary and run our fingers over the beads in her honor, yet what does it all mean? Am I not worthy of entrance into their heaven if I do not do as they say?

I have taken the insults and felt the stones that have been thrown at me by the young of my village. A few of them have hit hard and bruised the flesh, as they were hurled by some of the older boys who do not understand me well. But, Lord, there is no pain that can match the loneliness I have encountered here. The stones may just have been a welcome feeling for me, as they do not hurt as much as what I am feeling this day. I have a feeling of a hole in my heart that will cause me to lie dead where I once stood. I was able to ward off the broken bones and the scars of the switch inflicted upon my flesh. It was the words that cut to the bone and left the damage behind. I forgive them all, for they are not worthy of the wrath that would have befallen them had my father been there to protect me. The death he would have granted them, or the pain he would have inflicted upon them for treating me that way, would be horrid. He alone would cover my body with his to shield me from their attacks. It would never come to pass again. Oh, I miss him so.

I will pray to Mary more this day than I did in the past, for she alone will show me the way I must go. I believe in her so. I will not travel to the wall today or sit and watch the clouds this day. No, I must learn about why I am here. This is something I must do alone, for in the end, aren't we all just standing in front of our Lord and his gates of heaven truly alone. I have few I can turn to, yet there are many here of my ilk. I must recite the lessons taught to me by those who are so pious. Yet they still will dine alone behind the great doors.

We will continue to eat from our small campfires. We are no longer allowed to build the great ceremonial fire circles. They say they are pagan and against God's way. Why is this so? If Mary wants me to come to her, why are we not the same? I fear that these men of the black robes may not be who they say, for they seem different to me here.

They have taught me that I must obey them, for they are the ones chosen to make us all within their image. I have forsaken my adopted family and fled a great distance without the advantage of my sight to guide me here. I relied on men of another tribe to escort me here, yet I barely knew their names. I have trusted them, and yet I sit alone. Why is this so? I have been told to trust them, yet they show little in the way of trust toward us. Why is this so?

I shall walk to the river and watch the rafts and canoes as they come and go. Is there anyone from my ancestral village of Caughnawaga who may have arrived this day? I seek my friends and family, for I feel ill and alone. I will pray for peace in my heart, but I am not so worthy. There has been little in the way of word or show of anyone I know since I arrived. My journey was long, and I tolerated it in hopes that I had made the choice to lead a life of the women here and be among then in daily prayers and loyalty to the Lord above.

I sorrowfully long for the great fire circles with the drums and the songs of the elders. They have yet to come here, and I can only hear their voices if I sit here and listen to what the wind tells me. Oh, I miss them so. There are people here I can turn to, of course. I believe no one means me harm, but there is no family to talk to, or visit, or sit and talk of the Lord with. Oh, the walls of their fortification hold in the thoughts of those who have walked into its gates and shut them behind. Can this be the only way we are to learn our lessons? Should I go and knock on the doors with a great stick so they can hear me? Or should I wait until the morning, when they will again be thrown open to allow us passage?

They have a great altar built upon the stone, but they did not build one for us. No, ours is barely enough to keep the wind and snows out of the shelter when it comes. I do not mind this, but they do not feel we are worthy. Ours is cut from the thin alders near the fields we have cleared to feed them. Theirs has the roof of tiles made from the clay we have dug for them along with the mud to make our cook pots. Ours has a thatch of the weak grasses and takes much effort to repair. My people know not of cutting the great logs and building of the flattened wood and stone. No, we are not their equals, yet we are taught to pray the same. Why is it this way?

Should I have stayed behind and taken the wrath of my uncle and his kind? He at least let us know where we stood with him. He would turn his back to me and refuse me to come to the meal if I took a day to pray to the Creator of all above. He does not understand my kind, or me, but he at least would walk through the village and seek out all of his people. There were times when he was patient and kind to me, and he did make me welcome in his hut. But if I prayed to Mary or you, Lord, he would become angry and did not hesitate to remove me from this place. Here, they choose whom they will allow speaking to them, and most here are dispatched to the fields or the wooded areas outside the realm of this city.

I do not wish them ill. I have no pain for them, but, Lord, it is written in your book that I must follow, but who is in the lead? I am here of my own will. I believe I am not so naive that they took great advantage of me. I came to hear them speak and was told I could only get closer to you should

I come here to this mount. But I now believe the place has little matter and I could be welcomed to your side from any place I roam. I know it is I who must seek you out, not that you would not know or care where I am. I believe you could reach out and touch me at any turn of the trail that leads to you.

I wish to find you, Lord, but I pray it is soon. My body is tired, but it is not the work or sight that fails me. I believe it is my own will that may make me fail to travel further. I am among many here, but why am I so alone? I will walk to my hut and close the flap of the great bear skin. It is time for me to stop this pitiful display and find my will once again. I have come a great way, but my journey has just begun. I will pray to Mary today and seek my mother's help in finding my way. I know they are watching over me, for I feel the weight of them upon my shoulder. It brings me to my knees as I lean to pray to you. Oh, Mother, I need you so. Today I have questioned my beliefs, and I no longer feel safe. Please come to me. I will remain here without food or drink until you appear to me and I can see your face.

As this day ends, you have not come. I am not sad, for I will begin my prayers again tomorrow before the sun should rise from its resting place. I will ask of him on high to send you to me again. I will again go to the cliffs and wait as I have these many days. Oh, it will be a glorious reunion when we shall sit again. Will you bring her with you, for I love her as much as you? Please send me a sign and I will prepare a feast for you. I will surround myself with the laughter of children so you will be able to find me, for I have grown since I saw you last. But the voices of these blessed children, so sweet and pure, will give you clear voices to follow all the way to me, for I shall surround myself with their joyousness. Oh, Mother, please come to me soon, for I know what I must do.

The cheerful voices of the children have awakened me from my sleep. They have come to me for the lessons I try to teach them. I do not force it on them, for it must be their choice, not mine, whom they will follow. I am trying to be a spiritual guide to each of them and will show the right path. Whether they choose to follow it is another matter, and one I wish to discuss with their parents or aunts. I, however, would not enjoy seeing them return to their villages without a good belief in their thoughts as to how they must treat others or we all may be doomed to repeat our ways.

The men of the uniform will surely come from across the great waters and kill us all if we do not change, for we have given them quarters here, and they now have more men than we do. They will fight with a long gun against the bow and hawk. It is not an even thing they do, and few of them will fall to your ways. So I hope the children will grow in the Lord's grace and become the people of the ways to his gate, not to the place to be doomed in the underworld. They tell me it is a place of torture and fire. Why would anyone purposefully want to go there? I do not surely know. I will do everything I can to stay out of this place. I will lie prostrate day in and day out, in all weather, to keep from being chosen to go there to live. I will help with our children, and as they learn their prayers, they, too, will escape its dreadful bonds. I am a woman of God. I know, and I must do all I can to show them, I am worthy. Then he will know that I, too, can gain a place with him in his heaven. I know this from what I have been taught by them, but do they really believe it is so, or is it all just to have us come here to help with the children and the crops? Mother, please come to me this night and tell me it isn't so!

I will go to the wall again tomorrow and see if I can gain entry. I am not one they should fear. I am just a child of Jesus and one who loves his mother Mary so, and all I ask is that I, too, be allowed to journey to them when it is my time. I feel my time is certainly growing nearer, and I must watch for the signs that I am being called home to him. Oh, I look forward to the day when all of my earthly chores will be done, and I will be lifted above the clouds to live in a special place with no more sickness or death and sorrows, but I still have some things to do here.

The children who follow me must hear their lessons and say the beads I have made for them. I, for one, have a simple prayer for the youngest, and I recite it whenever they draw nearer to me. I have heard it before from the older Jesuits who first came to my village, and then it was lost to me. I listened to the good father this morning as he spoke the words, and it came flooding back to me as if I had never forgotten it. Oh, it is so sweet a prayer I shall add it to my daily prayers from this day forward. I say the words and the eyes of these children are upon me. I see their mouths in movement to the words as if they must learn it today.

I will say it often enough that they will have the time to add it to their prayers as well. I will say it in the cornfields and at the river's edge. I will say it at the top of the hills as I enter the forest, and I will say it again as I draw the water from the spring to replenish the body and the soul.

Oh, Mary, Mother of God, hear my simple words that I wish to share with all those who are near.

Remember, O most gracious Virgin Mary,
That never was it known that anyone who fled to thy protection,
Implored thy help, or sought thy intercession was left unaided.
Inspired with this confidence,
I fly to thee, O Virgin of virgins, my Mother;
To Thee do I come; before thee I stand, sinful and sorrowful.
O, Mother of the Word Incarnate,
Despise not my petitions,
But in thy mercy, hear and answer me.
Amen.[1]

I will ask the good father about these words, and some I still do not understand, but I have time yet to teach it to those little ones and learn what all it says. I think it reminds me best of my mother, who is with Mary this very day. Oh, I wish she would come for a visit. I could use her assistance this day with the children, for it is easy to get them to pray, but some need more time than others. I feel the boys will run to the wood and not return till the darkness follows them home again. It is the same with those who follow their chiefs and not the Lord. Our ways are good, and I feel most are just. We have been here for thousands of their years without repent. The black robes have taught us the way to reach the

---

[1] This is an actual seventeenth-century Catholic prayer.

Creator, and I, for one, will follow their lead. These children have seen much joy, and some have seen death on their trails. I want to take the pain away and have only my faith to guide me in this chore. How will they learn all that I have to teach? I must stay here for a while until they have heard it all. I will start them on their journey to God tomorrow, but today I must repent for my sins. I have not been worthy of the attention that Mary, my mother, has brought upon me.

They all now will follow me down to the river's edge, as I see a boy who has been sent to catch some fish. I tell him of the story of Jesus and how he, too, was a fisherman's son. The boy listens and even smiles as I begin the tale. He waits for a moment and then casts his net again into the boil of fish below him. Then he pounces into the waist-deep waters and captures a great deal of them within his net. But they all run out through the hole he has left in the net, from it rubbing on the great rocks along the banking. He again climbs out of the water and then throws the net into the water without the benefit of a leader, and it is soon lost in the current. I tell him of all the people who follow those who do not know the way and are lost. He looks at me again, but I see the eyes of a warrior on a mere boy, and I must step back. I speak to him of the Bible and how he should become a fisher of men.

His answer to me is, "I doubt you have enough herbs, woman, to make them taste as good as the fish there."

And with that, I say I hope I never have to find out, but the fish are swimming free, so neither of us will ever know for sure. He smiles and moves away. His younger brother falls in behind him, and they head to the trail back to the village. It is now afternoon, and the children tire of my rants, and they, too, fall by the wayside as we walk the great distance to the village. As we approach, the supper fires have already been lit.

It is late, and all is now coming to a calm I have not heard in so long. The children have gone to their huts and will fall quickly into a deep sleep from a busy day. Oh, Mother, I now understand why I am here. I have been summoned by you and the Lord to this place of the wide waters to teach them your ways. I love you so and want to honor you by doing what is asked of me. I know that if I was in the walled city, I, too, would not be able to bring the children together through the great distractions and abundant ways. I, too, have been chosen to say the words of the Jesuits and spread his word among our people. Many are from the Huron camp, some from the eastern villages, and us few of the Mohawk and Onondaga Tribes, but we are all God's children, I am told.

I, for one, will search them out to teach them the way to a better life. I will tend the sick. I will help the feebleminded, and I will assist with the births of our true hope. But best of all, I will become a good Christian and earn the way to heaven. That is why I am here. It is as if the clouds have cleared and I now can see my vision for a far distance.

As I sit here taking in all the abundance the Lord has surely provided, I see a small group of the children rolling down the hill just below me. I know their names to the last, but there is no need to disturb them, as they finally have broken from their lessons with the nuns to discover the joy of all his creations. The laughter is contagious, and I, too, am tempted to run down the hill and roll all the way to the bottom. I will not do so, of course, but it still is fresh in my memories of the rolling hills above us at Ossernenon and my childhood home. Oh, how that is a good a memory I wish to carry until my last day here.

One by one, they tumble, and one by one, they pick themselves up and run to the top of the hill to begin again, always in the same order, boy and girl, playing and laughing. Then I spy the smallest, a girl of no more than four, sitting halfway down the hill and crying as if a limb has been torn from her. I descend my hill and come up to the peak of theirs, and as all good children, they wait for me to get close and scatter like the pack of dogs rambling through the back fields.

She is sitting there as if made of stone, yet the weeping continues. And she raises up her arms and stretches them in my direction. Her given name is Wassana, yet they of the black robes call her Lily, and she is my favorite. Her cries are now just sobbing that flows like her tears. I comfort her and bring her cool waters from the spring and wash her face with it. She shows little sign of her encounter with the hill except a goodly scraped knee and a little mouse under her left eye. I suspect she will live. She is so beautiful and shows that she has been well treated, especially by our cooks.

As we continue to sit in the shade of the large chestnut tree, we have a great vantage point to watch the scampering of those who deserted her on the hill. They have followed the porcupine trails all the way down to the river's edge, and we last see them as they wade into its cool waters. As I begin to softly say a prayer, she looks up at me with those bright brown eyes, and they are searching my face and almost burn my flesh with their gaze. Her lips show her inner self, however, as she wears a cautious smile.

I look away and continue to say the words I have been taught, and she is calm and relaxed in my arms. In a moment, I dare to look upon her face again. Her tears have all dried away, and she has fallen fast asleep. She has no more cares in her world this day. Oh, how I long to be like her. How can I regain that peace that is born of the child? Oh, Lord, how can I teach them and be a fisher of men as it says in your book? I haven't lived with a family for a long time. Oh, I feel I am not worthy, but if I do not go forward with your plan for me, how will I, too, be saved? How will I do all that needs for me to do in such a little time? How will it all get done?

As I look upon her sweet face once again, I find she is looking at me and following my eyes with hers. She is silent yet saying so much to me. The wonderment about her is refreshing to me. Oh, to begin again, what a special thing we all have! We just need to find the right path to follow. I, for one, feel she has taught me far more this day than I could ever have taught her. Oh, Lord, it is about your children, isn't it, and we are all of one village. Don't they know this must be true? I know now my sorrowful lot in life. I am here to teach them all in the way of the nuns and to be as faithful as each of the Jesuits.

Oh, it has been a long day to be alive, yet it isn't nearly done. I will lift this child of God and carry her to her mother's house. Then I will begin to prepare the meal for those yet to return from their toils of this day. Some I can see in the light, and others will surely follow the glow of the campfires. The feast will be a bounty, for this night, I know my purpose, and all will rejoice in my happiness. Oh, what a beautiful sight as the mother and child melt to the robes, holding each other. They sit just inside the opening of the hut, and as I turn to depart, I hear the words "thank you" and "praise be to you." Yes, I have chosen the correct trail to follow, and I am firmly upon its well-worn path, for I know now this is the right way for me to go. I hear her final words: "I will pray to Mary for your salvation." Oh, what beautiful words.

I, for one, will accept all the prayers I can for my salvation, for I know it is a heavy burden to gain entry in his place. I will stop short of my own hut and pray for their souls as well. Mary and Mother will know for whom I speak. I hope they come for a visit with me tonight. It would be so good a time for them to appear.

I look toward the heavens, and I can see all the stars above as they run past this night's moon. The city of the Frenchmen appears to be all tucked in for the night. The great doors through which they pass are closed to us of this village. I will have to wait until tomorrow to gain the entry I seek. Yet I hear their laughter carried on the night's winds as it coolly breezes by me. The sound of their strings and joyful singing is a wonderful time to witness. Yet we cannot be with them, and this, I pledge to change. My voice is not as melodious as some, but I can so easily remember the words as they ring constantly in my ears. The traders are allowed, as are those who carry the trade from the faraway villages to our new home. What news do they have of my castle and my people? Oh, I miss them so. Who has gone beyond the living, and who has been born a new child? This is a good thing to hear, for I have been so lonely for them all. Even the braves who beat me are missed, for I do wish they would change their ways, and I pray often for them as well. I hope to see them all someday in the next world, but I, for one, hope they do not carry the stones with them!

Oh, Mother, I miss you so. I have been looking for you for a long time now. I have worried I would be sleeping when you come, and you would not wake me. Has Brother grown since the last visit? Is he yet a man? Has Father looked upon his village and smiled again? Oh, I hope he has seen the children. He would be so proud of them. Is Mary as beautiful as I remember her to be? Oh, I hope she comes to visit with you too. I will just close my eyes for one moment tonight.

Please do not allow me to miss you again, for I must visit with you one more time. I fear I will wake in a new place and you may not be able to find me. The wind has a bit of a chill this eve. I will wait by the fire, if you do not mind. I enjoy watching it send its fireflies into the sky. I wish I could follow them, for I do not know where they go. I had a busy day, and until all becomes bright in the world again, I will close my eyes. I worry about my faith and my inner desires, but thinking of you has helped make me believe I have chosen the right way to go.

My eyesight is failing me, Mother. My flesh has been scarred and torn, my back has been bent by the toil I enjoy, and yet my mind is as clear as the fresh snows. I am here for a better purpose, I am sure of this. I wake each morning to repeat the chores I did yesterday. I begin with the prayers you taught me, Mother. Then I say those of the priests. I remember the laughter and times long ago when we were a family, long before you all left this world and Mary motioned you to follow. There will be a day when we will sit around our own fire circle and sing and dance again. I will enjoy this time, for I have waited for it every day I have been alone. But I am not in such a hurry, as much as it hurts, for I am here for the children and must prepare their daily lessons.

Oh, the nuns do a fine job of teaching us what they feel we need, but I, for one, believe there is so much more. We know of their birthplace so far away, but they know little of our homes, and it is upon them they stand. How can they teach us anything until they know us well? I suppose the children are easier for them because they have only been here for a short time, but they, too, have been here before and will possibly come again. Those members of the Turtle Clan understand this from creation, but they will not learn this here. Oh, will they allow me to tell the stories of my lodge, or will I be prepared to teach them only what the black robes want them to know? Is this a good way to begin such a journey?

I know I will learn the ways to get into heaven and be with you again. My eyes may be failing, but not my will. I have again felt you in my heart this day, and the hole is now filled.

Chapter X
In the Light of a New Moon

The days of my life are clearly limited. We have so few of them to look back upon before they call our names to enter the gates of heaven. I hope and pray that those I have wasted or spent languishing in sadness are not too many. I wonder if he will count any of those times against me when we finally meet. I am looking forward to seeing his face and speaking with him soon enough, but there is still so much to do.

I have toiled the longest of times in the fields and in the making of the children's clothes from the trade cloth to keep my hands busy. It is little for me to do to make up for my body's weakness, and my oh-so-terrible eyesight. My poor health has prevented me from working the way I should. I realize they are only part of what has caused me to fall behind those of my village again. I sit here in my hut at times while they are still out working in the fields and at the fire circles, preparing the evening meal. So it is up to me to rise and begin while the moon is still full above me. I have tried to make up for my faults in my own way. But I know it will never make amends for all those slack times and when I was idle and not in prayer. Please forgive me, Lord. I only wish to repent for my sins.

It is my hope that with my sacrifices and special prayers, just maybe Jesus will see it as a way to forgive me and call me to his home just the same. This, I do not know for sure.

I know not of his plan for me either, but he took my infant brother and my mother, who was cradling him. And even my father was stricken with the cough, and he was as big a man as I have ever seen. The good Father Lamberville told me that he has taken them all away to his paradise a long time ago and that they are happy in heaven. The Lord's kingdom is a wonderful place, and it is open to all who believe in him. I did not get to say goodbye to them and long to speak to them all once again. I know they are in a better place, but the ache in my heart of losing them has never lessened to this day. I feel them with me at every step I take. Each time I look to the sky, I have a feeling they are looking down at me and smiling. Yet I feel the need to reach out and be able to touch them once again. I must find out for sure that they are no longer in any pain and are without fear. Will I again be able to greet them? Will they know me in this body and not as the young child I was when they left?

All I will have to do is to hear the Lord's voice calling out to me in the twilight, or even in the brightness of this day, as I will continue to be quietly waiting for him. I am sure I am ready. He must know where I am, as he can hear all and see all we mortals say and do. We cannot hide from him even in the deepest of the caves or thickness of the forest. He will appear to me wherever I am. I have been taught this by the Jesuits and the sisters. And they have no reason to lie to me. All that I have learned has prepared me for this special moment.

I, for one, cannot wait to hear his call. It will be a sweet voice, I am sure of this. It fills the air with such a wondrous sound that no one else has ever heard. They of the sisters' house tell me I will hear the angels singing and a great ceremony will unfold, the likes of which I have not seen before. The sky will be as beautiful a blue as I have ever seen and as clear as the stream we used to fish from when we were mere children.

I have been to many of the ceremonial fire circles set in the center of our village and love to watch the ancestors' faces appear in the flames. I saw them as they raced swiftly skyward and disappeared into the darkness far above the last sparks. Many, I did not know, and they were gone so quickly I could not ask my aunt if she saw them as well. Many seemed to be in pain, and their faces all showed a great deal of sorrow. I prayed for them as they flickered by me.

Our people's beliefs go back to the Sky Woman, and she guided us for such a long time. Her beginning of the earth made sense to us, as we knew no other—but I am told it is not his way. When he wants you to join him, he calls out your name, and you just appear in front of him before you can change your mind. I have been told many times, we cannot resist. Then, as you stand there at his feet, you will see everything that you have ever done in your life come before you as clearly as if it were today. He will judge you alone by the deeds you have done on his earth. The good as well as the bad ones are how he will determine if you enter his realm. I have seen the pictures of the angels blowing their horns. Oh, what a wondrous sight to behold. I bet it will be a most beautiful time. I hope I get to witness it soon. I am, after all, so ready to join him. I do not know why he is waiting to call on me, but it is not for me to ask him. Today would be a good day to go, but tomorrow I must teach the children again. Maybe he will wait until I know so much more of his ways.

I am just a native princess and do not have all the wisdom of my mother or her aunts. I have tried my best to study the book of the priests and follow them in their Mass, yet I have been told I am not worthy of their convent, for I am an ignorant native. I try to be better than I am, but it is so hard.

The feeling here in my adopted village of Kahnawake is so joyous these days. But as the new settlers arrive, I still see the pain and the agony on their faces. Many have traveled from the farthest reaches to end up here from their so-distant villages. I enjoy greeting them one by one as they pass my hut, and I occasionally wait for them on the trailhead so they can give us words of our families. Oh so distant, the memories of the old villages have become. I have been here but for a few years, and yet it is fading from my thoughts. I must keep their memories alive somehow.

I have wondered of my own fate should I undertake a visit to my ancestral home in Ossernenon once again, but it is not a feeling of fear, for I am ready for all that is out there for me to see. It would be nice to return to the home of my aunts' and that of dead who watch over me. But I am told my uncle will serve me a blow that will send me to the netherworld to wander alone. This, I cannot let happen, not out of fear but out of my love for my Lord and Mary as well. I must be able to see them and give myself to them, for only they know my true future. I will stay here for now and forever, it seems, but it is not of my choice. I have been told by those who have come here by the canoa that the village of my birth has gone. It is no longer known to those who travel our rivers. The forest has claimed it and all about its fences except the souls who remain buried there.

My uncle built our new castle just a short way up the hills. His claim is that it is the birthplace of all the Iroquois. Our doubt of this grows quietly upon our lips, for he has shown us no proof. I cannot say if he is lying, but the elders shook their heads over and over again. Does he know something we do not? It is a good place that is high and dry, with a small field within the walls. A great spring is near, and the high cliffs of the hills protected us well enough. This is the place where I came to the Lord first. I played with the clay and glass of the Jesuits and left many in the dirt to see if they would grow. There was a time when all was not at peace as it is today. Many men came and went under the cloak of darkness, and we as a people bleed from the wounds.

It was my father who was the greatest of the chiefs, and we were the proudest of nations of the Mohawks. Today they seem to be so small in numbers. Everyone has been scattered among the new villages hidden deep in the forest. Even there, they do not grow in size as we did, as many of the men still do not return from the fishing and hunting camps. Maybe they succumb to the ball and patch of these new Frenchmen who kill for the prize of an ear or nose. Our axe and bow are silent against them.

There is many a squaw now who mourns in the privacy of the hut on the long nights when they realize they are to be alone. The children race from place to place, seeking out a father who will never teach them of the pond or stream, or the fight. They, too, will look to others but will come away short of the knowledge to survive as a people regardless of how hard they try. The native is a species that will not outlast the rest, for we are the ancient ones, and the young always learn to cull the old first before they move on to the young and end it all.

My time has been pleasant enough with the children to care for, yet I feel there is a greater purpose for me, and I must end this earthly journey to find its destiny.

I sit here today, darning the robes I will wear at the end of it all. It will be a white robe of many beads and colors. I have few of my mother's things, for she has been gone a long time now, yet my aunts collected some of her possessions and handed them to me as I began my wait. Oh, I will see them all soon enough, and for this, I shall be forever grateful. Yet the children have grown now and gone to raise their own children and tend their own houses. It is not that I wish to go early in my time, but it is as if I just have no other choice. When I raise myself from the blankets of fur in the early light, I can sense that I have little left to give to my earthly family. My back is bent, and I have lost even more of my sight. I can still make it to the fields and will do so until

I have no breath left in my body to go forward. But for now, I must pause here and wait for my strength to return.

In the beginning, I was a child who never really knew my parents. All I have learned is from my aunts and the chief who has been the father to me since the early days. He does not appreciate my feelings and was constantly trying to have me taken by the young men of his village. He has also brought in the trappers from the French to court me, but I have no interest in them.

I have overslept this morning, and there cannot be any excuse for that. I will make a penance this evening for this indiscretion. I must not become lazy, for it is sinful. The sun is nearly over the hills, and soon it will be in full view. There are chores to get to, and I have again become a slacker. I will add to the coals I will carry away from the fire, as I must make amends. Their pain is nothing I cannot handle, so please show me no mercy. Those of the village should not have to take up for me. Even when I am feeling less than myself, it is my task to do. They have been given enough of their own.

The sunlight is now filtering through the trees, and it is sending a beautiful shadow through the early-morning fog. Oh, this is a wondrous time of the day. It is simply magical. My head is spinning as if it is a child's toy. I cannot see the ground in front of me nor feel my footsteps as I lay them down. I can feel the warmth of the sun as it caresses me, but there seems to still be a chill in the morning air. I should not rest, but I cannot go any further. The trail has become too difficult for me to travel this day. I will rest just a moment. I will kneel in prayer, and all will be right again, I am sure of this. I must not let the others down. It will burden them so.

I have fallen in my own tracks that I have worn into deep ruts in the earth. They extend all the way to the fields. I'm afraid I cannot stand by myself now and have little breath to yell out. But still I see for assistance. I hear the laughter of the children off in the distance now, but none will venture near. The joyous no one—is this my fate? Will they find me someday lying here as others go by this place on their way to the work? Will the animals disburse my bones along the forest floor, all without a care for who I once was?

I can hear my labored breath now. It is an odd sound. Its raspy voice is drowning out the world around me. Yet I can clearly see the wondrous shapes of the clouds as they reform over my head. I cannot remember them being this beautiful before. The veil over my eyes seems to have been lifted, as he must be allowing me this beautiful view.

The faces I see above me cause me no fear at all. They all are familiar in some way. I shall be happy to just lie here and wait for him to come claim me. I hope he can recognize this weakened husk of one of his faithful. I am so not worthy of his love, but I know no other.

My vision is cured now, and as if by the magic of a shaman, I can also hear the distant waterfall as it splashes into the pool so far away. It is clean and crisp. A young fawn silently bends a knee to capture a quick drink and struts away without a care. I want for the coolness of its waters, and I'm reminded of my own baptism, now seemingly so long ago. I see the crow showing me the way home again, yet I cannot rise to follow him any longer. He will have to go on and alert

192

the others to what is happening here. I'm afraid to close my eyes for the fear of missing something. Everything around me is so vivid, without a flaw. Oh, it is so peaceful and beautiful now. I do not wish to rise from this spot again. No, please do not help me. Let me lie here a little longer. I have never seen his world this way before, and it is truly wondrous to behold. Oh, I will miss this all, yet I am not afraid to finally know what he has in store for me. I hear it is even more beautiful once you are with him and there is no sickness, no pain. Everything will last as long as the sky itself.

I hear the thumping of my own heart now, and it is slow yet steady. The sound does not drown out all that is around me. It mixes with all the others and makes a soothing, almost-cooing sound. This is bringing me in closer to my dreams. My heart's beating is the most beautiful drum I have ever witnessed. I can hear the beetle as it walks by me, and even the lowly worm scratches at the earth as it passes me by. I hear the sounds of the ruffling of the leaves as they ready their flight. I can hear the wind calling out to me as if it is a whisper on a cool evening. I am finally so alive.

Dear Jesus, I see your face clearly now in the clouds, and I am ready to be judged. I have no demands of you, nor your Mother, as I have said all that I have to say when I knelt in my prayers. As I lie here prostrate, I see all those of my village surrounding me. What a beautiful sight is in front of me, with all the candles lit and the children sitting almost quietly in front of their parents, but why are they crying so? They should be happy for me, as I've been called home. I hear the faint din of the drum. It is such a beautiful sound. The sisters are kneeling with their beads pressed against their chests, and I know these prayers they are silently saying. May I join you? Just give me a minute to catch my breath and I will again kneel in prayer. Oh, the mystery I have waited so long to discover is about to unfold. All has been made ready.

Yes, Mother Mary, I am ready now. May I take your hand? The warmth of your touch has brought a glow to my face again. It is such a beautiful feeling. I have no pain or fear, for I recognized you when I first saw your face in the beautiful light. We have spoken many times, and you are an old friend to me. Welcome to my meager home.

Today I will be reunited with my brother and my dear mother. Father will be along soon, and all will be right again. I am ready.

Jesus, I love you!

END

In the year of the Lord 2017, a young maiden from a time
and place of little-known history has risen through her
virtue to sainthood.
Because of her miracles and her faith, we are all the better for
having her amongst us.

Please feel free to send an e-mail and tell us what you think of
our collaboration.

Dan "Bishop" Feeney
bishopstudio68@gmail.com

Bishop Feeney has other novels and short stories that are interesting, informative and a fun read. Please keep an eye out for one of his many works that will include these listed below and others:

The King of Pumpkin Knob
Dead Reckoning
The Voyaging
Tumblehome
The Spirit of Ecstasy
The Rowboat
The Nottingham Galley

Thank you

Made in the USA
Middletown, DE
19 December 2021

54413240R00123